Wafting Earthy

Fragrances from All Over the World

WriteFluence

Cover Illustrator: Vibhuti Bhandarkar

The beauty of fragrance is that it speaks to your heart and hopefully someone else's.

ELIZABETH TAYLOR

Contents

Preface

We thought about announcing a story-writing contest to congregate the best stories from all over the world; and PenFluenza was born!

To make sure we get literary entries that were worthy of reaching a wider reader base, and the writers are fairly judged for their writing skills; we began our jury-hunt and were soon lucky enough to have found Ms. Susmita Bagchi and Ms. Anupama Dalmia; both adept in the field of literature and contributing to it since years. Both the judges graciously and unconditionally accepted to be our jury for their love for literature, and we shall forever be grateful to them for the same.

When we decided on the theme 'Fragrances'; little did we know that we would receive a whopping 142 story submissions on the prompt most of which were also following all the participation guidelines.

In due course of time, the contest received attention from numerous bloggers, literary organisations and writers not only from India, but from all over the world. PenFluenza became our first international short-story writing contest and almost a signature mark for us. While we shortlisted the top stories which were later judged by our jury; it was a very tough decision to make with each story written thoughtfully and every plot trying to convince us in its own way to be better than the rest.

Here's what our jury had to say about the stories they read:

Susmita Bagchi: "Each of the stories are one better than the other. The theme, the language and the choice of words is excellent. It was really difficult to judge them. The more I read them over and over again, judgement became all the more difficult. Expressions have improved over the years and the depth of their writing shows how deeply the writers think and how much the theme means to them."

Anupama Dalmia: "It was a pleasure reading such wonderful stories. I enjoyed them all and it is amazing how the prompt resulted in a variety of story ideas. My best wishes to the participants and Team WriteFluence."

With great pleasure, we bring together the winning stories of our very first short-story contest PenFluenza which was organised by us in January 2021.

Acknowledgements

Thank you to all the writers who have helped WriteFluence shape into the entity that we are, to all the writers and the participants without whom PenFluenza would not have been a success.

Special thanks to **Vibhuti Bhandarkar** for having designed the best cover we could have had the stories all wrapped into!

Many thanks to our respected jury who helped us pick the most impeccable fragrances for Wafting Earthy!

About our jury

Susmita Bagchi has been an educationist for more than four decades and has primarily been teaching English and Geography as a Secondary School teacher, to children from Grades 8 to 10. With her 45 years of immaculate expertise over the language, she has imparted knowledge across ICSE, CBSE and SSC boards. She has helped shape and brighten the future of many, and has worked in globally recognized and renowned schools across India viz. Renukoot and Lucknow (Uttar Pradesh), Bhubaneshwar (Odisha), Mumbai (Maharashtra) and in Dubai (UAE) and has also trained students for Grade 12 Exams & GRE. Bagchi is a very well-read person and her favorite reads include all classics of Charles Dickens, all books of P.G. Wodehouse, Daniel Steele, Sydney Sheldon, Robin Cook & many others. The book that's currently on her bedside table is The Algebra of Happiness by Scott Galloway.

After years of guiding students, Bagchi has not hung up her boots and is now a Certified Holistic Health Coach. She helps patients suffering from various auto immune health problems, heal. Her journey of learning continues while she pursues another Cancer-related course from the Pennsylvania University.

Bagchi's WriteFluencing Mantra is: "Personal experience broadens one's perspective and varied reading opens one's mind & understanding – That influences what one writes and how one expresses."

Anupama Dalmia is a 30-time award winning blogger, author, serial entrepreneur with three ventures, social influencer, creative writing mentor, choreographer and mother to a 6-year-old. She is a Karamveer Chakra (Silver) awardee which is a Global Civilian Honour presented by International Confederation of NGOs in association with the United Nations. She is a Sheroes Champion where she motivates a community of 15 million women and is also an Amazon approved Influencer. She has been featured among the top bloggers and influencers of India on multiple leading platforms and her journey has been covered by coveted media like Official Humans of Hyderabad, The New Indian Express, Femina, The Better India, Women's Web, TOI Group, Influglue, Youth Ki Awaaz and YourStory to name a few. She is the only Indian who has been nominated in the category of "Digital Transformation" by Global Digital Women which is a Berlin based International network of female digital pioneers at the Digital Women Leader Awards 2020. In 2020, she was conferred with the Sarojini Naidu International Award for Women 2020 for her contribution in the field of writing, social work and entrepreneurship. Her literary works have been published on leading magazines, platforms and newspapers of India. She has also contributed to International Literary Journals and her poems, blogs and fictional stories have been widely appreciated.

She's currently reading "Unaccustomed Earth" by Jhumpa Lahiri.

Dalmia's WriteFluencing mantra is "Be honest to your writing and the connection will happen"

Memaroma

By Tanvi Kashyap

I remember reading a story of a mother with one eye. Her son felt embarrassed because of her eye only to realize at the end of her life that she had sacrificed it because he was born with a defective one. It is indeed true, that we realize much later, how unconditional her love is. Right now, standing outside her door, about to ring the bell, I am praying, yearning to let her know what she means to me. The doorbell is answered by Michelle, my mother's nurse.

"Thank goodness you are here. She has refused to come out of her room and is not eating anything", said Michelle, trying hard to sound cheerful, but failed to hide her perturbation.

"Let me see", I replied apprehensively. I stepped inside and walked through the hallway. My heart started beating really fast. It was heartbreaking to see her in that condition.

As I entered her room, she reacted just as I had expected.

"Go out from here! Who are you? Where is my family? Please leave. I don't want to see you again", she blurted out. My heart was pounding really fast, I felt totally helpless and tears welled up in my eyes. It all started two years ago. Alzheimer's entered her life unsolicited and changed our lives forever. Losing one's loved ones, changes our lives to such an extent that the will to live just vanishes somehow, or maybe something so painful happens in life that we just wish to erase our entire memory.

Alzheimer's disease is a neurological condition in which the brain cells die and the patient suffers from memory loss. My mother was living alone in this house with a full-time nurse. I was living just two blocks away with my husband. Her deteriorating health was a major cause of concern for me which compelled me to take leave for weeks only to attend to her needs and spend time with her. Unfortunately, she could not recognize me at all. She ate her dinner after sometime and finally slept like a baby. But my eyes were full of sleeplessness and despair. I just couldn't figure out a way to help her. I randomly started searching on the internet, but even after an hour, couldn't find any worthwhile solution. In all this bewilderment, I completely forgot about something. It was Mom's birthday the next day. Immediately, I rushed into the kitchen, brewed some fresh coffee beans and started baking my mother's favorite mocha cheesecake.

Luckily, I found almost all the ingredients in the pantry. In half an hour, the whole apartment was filled with the aroma of this ambrosial gateau.

The incident that happened after that was not less than a miracle. I could not believe my eyes. Mom came out of her room, constantly repeating these words, "My cheesecake is ready. I think I have put some extra bit of coffee into it, otherwise it smells perfect."

I could not believe my ears. It took me sometime to understand what had happened. "Well, of course it does!" was my joyous reaction.

Eureka! My happiness knew no bounds. I had finally found a way to help mom get her memory back. This smell had reminded her of a little incident that had happened twenty years ago, when she had baked a coffee cheesecake and made the same mistake I made. The aroma of the cake was so evocative. I am clearly able to recall and understand my French lessons now.

'La Madeleine de Proust', the smell of a madeleine (a French tea cake often thought of as a cookie) made the writer Marcel Proust reminisce old events. Suddenly the anger my mother had on her face every time she looked at me was gone for a while. She happily enjoyed the cake thinking that she had baked it. This was the first time in the past two years that I witnessed a positive development. My heart was full of hope and optimism. She slept again, but I just could not sleep any more. It felt like I had so much more to do.

Eager to explore this new found discovery, I searched on the internet about this incident that intrigued me so much. I found out that various fragrances and aromas are evocative and remind us of our past life events. Every time it rains, it reminds me of a trip we had to the south during monsoons when I was 8 years old. While sleeping, a person's mind is very relaxed and thus, in its natural state, bringing back memory can be much easier using redolent smells. I was really excited to take over this venture and give a new life to my mother.

My next task would be to recall events from my childhood that involved some fragrances that can make her nostalgic. I started looking for my diary in which I used to write every memorable incident that ever happened during my childhood hoping to find some clues as to which fragrances can be used. I opened drawers after drawers, but couldn't find anything useful. After searching for a long time, I finally found something which might help as well, but it was not my diary. It was my mother's diary, of the year 2001. I prayed to God to forgive me for reading my mother's diary, and with a little hesitation I opened it. My mother's love for words and wisdom whiffed out of every page that she had written and of course her love for her only child as well. I was so glad I came across this diary. I could read her heart out. There was this one particular excerpt which caught my attention and I decided that this could be really helpful in bringing my mother's memory back. There was a certain smell deeply etched on her memory. Before I realized, it was dawn already. I opened my window and welcomed dewy floral scented wind with utmost warmth. Indeed, it was going to be a memorable day.

I got ready immediately as there was no point in sleeping now. I had to plan for my mother's big birthday surprise. I just had a few hours to prepare everything. The countryside was a two-hour drive and my destination was waiting for me there. I had already called up Mr. Becker and gave all the necessary instructions. A few hours later, two trucks full of a refreshing surprise were on their way to meet mommy. My heart was pounding fast now, if nothing happens the way I intend, at least this will make her feel extremely happy and Il get a chance to express my heart. We reached home by afternoon during my mother's nap time, the perfect time for me to set up everything. Four of us were working at full tilt. Yes, I took help from Michelle and the two truck drivers. After two hours of running here and there in my mother's garden, planning and executing haphazardly, we finally finished the task with perfection. I stepped back and looked at the beautiful arrangement. It was splendid, such a captivating sight. The essence of it all was the fragrance, fresh, delicate and reminiscent.

Michelle went inside to invite mother to witness the grandiose, as I was too overwhelmed to do anything. My mother came outside, and could not believe her eyes. Floribunda, Grandiflora, Groundcover, Polyantha, Alba, Old garden, Hybrid tea, wild pink, snow white, crimson, orange, blue. The fragrance, the arrangement was the same as my parents had it thirty years ago in their farmhouse. It was a miracle to have it all assembled in just a few hours. My parents had always been fond of planting roses. We had a beautiful rose garden in our farmhouse nurtured and cared with diligence and commitment. We have made so many unforgettable memories in that garden, playing there all day and then lying down on the grass looking at the stars. Dad narrating his favorite stories and life was indeed a bed of roses. Mom had tears in her eyes.

The sight and the fragrance had brought back something inside her soul, she knew deep down inside that this was familiar. Love and emotions touch our heart and soul so deeply that it can defy memory loss. I looked at her with all the love I had for her and our eyes met. She cried and cried. All of us were in tears. I embraced her. I don't know whether she could finally feel that I was her daughter or not, but I was sure that she didn't care anymore. Her soul was speaking to her now, and it is omniscient.

As soon as the sun had set, we were lying down on

the grass and watching the stars. "You should come every day. I will teach you how to nurture these blooming beauties. This fragrance reminds me of a deep connection I have with this garden and..", she stopped abruptly.

"And?" I interrogated.

"... and you".

Winner, Winner!

By Victoria Fenwick

"**G**ood things never happen to me," Henrietta thought, tucking a plume of red hair behind her ear. She shifted uneasily on the hard, steel chair. She was the only one in the waiting room. The room itself was almost entirely bare, save for a scattering of metal stools, two chrome coffee tables, a large flashing clock and an empty receptionist's desk.

For the fifth time, she examined her voucher and tried to let it sink in. Embossed in gold calligraphy was the enticing offer: 1 free sixty-minute massage at Lefour Spa! For as long as she had worked and lived on the farm, there were regular competitions to reward the most diligent employees. Henrietta had long been hoping for the day that her bosses would finally notice her dedication and whisk her off to be pampered and preened. But now that she was here at the spa, perching on the edge of her seat, she only felt nervous and uncomfortable.

The clock on the wall behind the desk flashed the time: 01:30. Wrinkling her nose, she checked her watch. That wasn't the time at all! It was 10 in the morning. She made a mental note to tell the receptionist that they had a faulty clock. Tapping her long nails gently on the arm of the chair, she inhaled deeply.

"I deserve this," Henrietta told herself. She worked hard on the farm, every day. There was no rest, no breaks, just constant foraging in the orchards, checking the feed and fresh water, running here, running there, running everywhere. Sighing as she looked down at her ragged nails, she noted the dirt embedded in the folds and cuticles and all the rough edges.

"I really need to look after myself more," she thought. Well, she was now in the right place. She deserved this, and she had earned this! Through her nose, she took another deep breath. What was that she could smell? It reminded her of her grandmother's roast dinners: warm and comforting.

"The receptionists must be on their dinner break," she concluded.

"Madam?" Her eyes snapped open and she sat up straight; she had started to drift off.

"Yes?" she replied, smoothing her hair in what she imagined was a discreet manner.

"They are ready for you, next door." The receptionist was dressed all in white and was standing there as if she had been waiting for some time.

As Henrietta rose to her feet, she saw the receptionist extend her arm toward her. "Allow me."

Before Henrietta could protest, she whipped off her down jacket and slung it over her arm. Turning with a click of her white heels, the receptionist motioned with her head in the direction of a corridor to the right side of the desk. "This way please."

Henrietta stood there, frozen, feeling exposed. Goosebumps tingled on her pale skin; she rubbed her arms and hurried after the receptionist. Down the dim corridor, she was led through a large frosted glass door into a private room where the masseuse welcomed her. It was decorated sparingly, much like the waiting room, with charcoal grey walls and a silver massage table. Gentle glowing lights on the ceiling imbued the room with warmth and a faint humming sound emanated from a fan at the back of the room. On the table rested a small head pillow and delicate, white towels folded neatly, waiting for her. The masseuse, who was sporting a clean white pinafore and cap, nodded politely and left the room, allowing her to change.

After kicking off her shoes, Henrietta removed her trousers and vest and hung them on a peg at the back of the room then lay face down on the table, arranging the towels to cover her back. She relaxed her shoulders and smiled, excited for the hour of sheer bliss.

Returning to the room, the masseuse removed the pillow and then guided her head into a hole with a padded rim. The towel on her back was lowered to rest across her tail bone and she felt his hands run up and down her body. Poking her in the hip, he grunted, "You're a little butterball, aren't you?"

Shocked, Henrietta opened her mouth to protest in offence, but the padded edges of the face hole pressed her jaw firmly together and muffled any attempt to reply. "We have lemon infused oil or honey. How does the honey sound?"

Henrietta gave the rude man a tentative thumbs up, and he gently placed her arm by her side.

"Honey it is then."

The sweet, heady, floral smell reminded her of home and her grandma who she missed terribly. She used to tend hives that thrummed with the busy sound of bees. Years ago, as a special treat, her grandma would give her honey toast in the morning. She remembered gobbling it up quick before her sisters could take it. They always fought over the scraps.

The masseuse's hands glided over Henrietta's back in a repetitive motion, kneading out the knots between her shoulder blades. The warm honey oil felt slick and smooth as it was rubbed into her skin. Memories of hot, sticky puddings and toffee-dipped apples floated to the surface of her memory carried by the thick aroma of syrup and lavender. She sighed with content. She remembered cozy suppers in the winter with the family huddled together, safe and snug, delightedly unaware of the snow storms burgeoning outside. Thoughts of hazy summer nights on the farm flickered then disappeared like the heat of a July day that rises and floats away. The tension she was holding in her back and neck melted and dissolved into nothingness. She never wanted to leave.

She snapped open her eyes again and felt an uneasy pang. She could no longer feel the sturdy hands working the muscles in her back. The room was almost silent apart from the fan, which was now droning angrily. Feeling sticky and rather hot, Henrietta nervously perched on her elbows and craned her head around. A flush of embarrassment rushed to her cheeks; 'I must have fallen asleep,' she muttered.

Beads of sweat formed on her brow as she pulled the towel around her body. Her skin prickled and flared uncomfortably; the room felt far too hot. She went to throw on her clothes that she had removed earlier but they were not hung neatly on the peg as she had left them - they were gone.

Panicking, she searched the room which was now unbearably hot. Scorching air seared the back of her throat and the hairs in her nostrils; her eyes felt like they were drying out. She tried blinking to ease the sting but they continued to water and burn, blurring her vision. Henrietta ran over to the door and threw her hands out in front of her. Frantically feeling, patting and groping around the hot glass, her chest grew tighter. Where was the handle? Her palms slammed against the searing Perspex panes. The fan was now whirring violently. She started yelling. Then banging. Then kicking. There was nobody there.

Squinting, she looked beyond the door, desperately trying to spot the masseuse or receptionist from before. She could see as far as the desk and the clock blinking behind it. It now flashed '60' in glowing red digits. But the room was as empty as when she first arrived.

Where did everyone keep going? Sweat ran down from her neck to her breast as red blotches appeared mottling her sticky skin. A wave of relief washed through her as two blurry figures appeared at the door. She recognized their white uniforms immediately.

"HELP!" She bellowed, thumping the foggy glass with her fist. Henrietta screamed her throat hoarse but the figures in white made no move to assist her, and just continued to stare curiously through the door.

"HELP!" She wailed again. It was so hot she was in pain. Her knuckles were almost raw from striking the torrid glass. Again, and again, she threw her shoulder into the door, crying and yelling.

"Why aren't they helping me?" Was she thinking or shrieking? The fan was almost deafening now. Why was it so loud?

"Does nobody realize I'm in here?" Helplessly, she sank

down to the floor and wept. From the floor, she could just about make out what the voices from outside were saying.

"Glazed..."

"...With honey "

"Should go nice and crispy..."

"...about an hour left"

With horror, Henrietta looked again through the misty pane of the door to the figures behind it, noticing their tall white hats and double-breasted button-down coats. Then, in front of her burning eyes, the door stretched horizontally, rolling lengthways until it engulfed the entire side of the room and she was faced with a gigantic, hazy wall of glass. She saw the orange lights, blazing above her, then she smelled the delicious aroma from before: the smell of dinner.

She looked down at her pink, plump, plucked body, now sizzling in agony, and screamed.

Jackfruit

By Anushree Bose

T he golden sun spilt across the cloudy sky like the nucleus of a poached egg oozes out upon teasing. The recently distempered lime green cottage of the Banerjees stood solemn in the sultry summer. Tall brick-walls secured its perimeter. The house itself resembled a handsome square-face with straight walls, a mahogany door for a mouth and two stained glass windows for eyes. From across the street, the foliage of jujube, guava, jackfruit and mango trees crowding the front yard looked like irregular bangs hugging the gable-roofed forehead of the cottage. Binodini liked this view of the house best. A little distance made it seem so welcoming and guileless!

On her first day, she had stood transfixed at the sight of this little nook of a paradise, sincerely hoping to make it her home. Relatives and neighbors had come to bless her on the occasion of her bodhu baran ceremony, bearing presents of gold, silver, silk, and brass. Bent forward, she had touched many wrinkled, weather-beaten feet with her right hand, and then pressed her fingers to her forehead painted with intricate designs drawn with sandalwood paste. The guests reciprocated by lightly patting her head, uttering blessings of fortune, fertility and husband's longevity, and feeding her an excessive amount of sweets. The latter made her retch. Her mother-in-law had ushered Binodini to the backyard with a vegetable patch for some fresh air as murmurs of disapproval broke into the living room. "Ah, the Banerjees got a delicate one!" as if Binodini was a custard apple, already too soft to last the season.

Binodini had been married for the good part of a year, and yet the aspersions persisted. Her mother, aunts and five married sisters had prepared her for the wedding but not for the marriage. Sure, she grew up learning household chores and doing harmless charms to sway the odds of receiving a good husband in her favor.

For sixteen consecutive Mondays, twice a calendar year, she subsisted only on water to be blessed with a husband like Shiva, the lord of Kailasha. She would lick off the sauce from a bay leaf which landed on her supper platter in the hope of chancing upon a caring mother-in-law. Much like birth, death and epidemics, weddings were ordained by divine will. Binodini had put her faith in the Gods above and did all that the elders asked of her. When the village match-maker brought the Banerjee's proposal to their doorstep, she believed it to be a payback for her fasts and good deeds. Her family sang how well off the Banerjees were, how she would live like a queen, have servants, eat delicacies, and be adored as the only son's bride. Could they be more wrong?

Sure, the Banerjee's had an electric mixer-grinder to her mother's stone mortar-pestle, colored television with a cable connection with paid channels to the black-&-white television with Doordarshan subscription at her poor headmaster father's. Here she had a whole almirah to herself that could fit twice the number sarees she owned, in contrast, at her father's Binodini had half a trunk's space that she shared with her mother. But try as she might, Binodini found no affection within these frigid walls. She was another installation to the house; acquired out of necessity and obligation to uphold the Banerjee's social standing.

As per etiquette, she was not to sit for supper or tea with her mother-in-law and father-in-law. However, neither her husband nor her sisters-in-law gave her company. She was always on the standby while others dined; to serve some more rice or gravy from the steaming pots and pans in the kitchen. She waited on everyone and ate alone at the imposing eight-seater rosewood dining table. Biju kaka, the cook-cum-bearer, ate when she did but his place was the kitchen's bare red iron-oxide floor. There was enough left for the two of them, always.

However, by the time it was Binodini's turn, unlike Biju kaka who ate his mound of rice and curries with gusto, Binodini had no appetite left. Breathing in the aroma of fish, meat and spices while cooking and serving food several times throughout the day, Binodini felt full even before she could chew a morsel. Binodini lurked by the kitchen door in the evenings, trying to catch snatches of conversations others were having while she fried some more fritters, refilled the platter of butter scones or replaced the kettle of tepid tea. Idling was forbidden. Many late afternoons she sat knitting woolen mittens, vests, mufflers and button-down cardigans beside her snoring mother-in-law who would inspect her handiwork soon after her siesta. When they ran out of knitting yarn, before Binodini could catch a breath, spools of thread were pulled out of chests. Binodini found herself crocheting doilies in a blink that would be part of the bridal trousseau for her three sisters-in-law.

Binodini's presence was as good as air: essential, invisible and inconsequential to the scheme of things in this microcosm. Her opinions died in her throat from suffocation as they could not be let out. What was the point of this unceasing drudgery? Preparing five-course meals she does not relish, doing laundry until her palms were raw, knitting and crocheting things she cannot use? Not a word of concern from her husband in public or private, who would be fast asleep long before she climbed into bed! Occasionally, she would lay like a log while he made urgent, feverish love to her resigned torso. The mornings following such torrid nights were the worst; her body's ache and mother-in-law wrath, both struck in unpredictable ways.

Binodini was as much in doubt of her recluse husband's affection as she was sure of her mother-in-law's spite. Her waking moments were crowded with orders, advice, admonishments and nit-picking from her mother-in-law. Though mostly quiet, the father-in-law spoke nicely to her, and that was all he ever did. Binodini often thought of running back to her father's but what would she say? There was more food than she could eat. The husband is distant, but men usually are. The sisters-in-law are friendly but not friends. The mother-in-law is severe but cannot be called cruel. The father-in-law is non-interfering and non-complaining, a bare presence. The in-laws gave her new clothes, never asked for dowry as promised and seldom mentioned her parents as if Binodini had dropped into their home straight from the old mango tree in the front yard. How would Binodini possibly explain her savage desire to drown herself in the

Ganges? Exhausted from the daily grind of menial chores and sapped out from corrosive ruminations, Binodini suddenly succumbed to deep sleep, like unwary children occasionally fall into open maintenance holes.

Merely minutes later, a commotion woke her up. Binodini drew the pallu of her saree over her head and approached the living room. It was three 'o clock in the afternoon, and the air indoors felt humid, sticky and thick with the odor of ripe jackfruit. A while ago, Biju had heard a loud thud. He ran to the front yard and found the precious fruit on the ground, its golden flesh oozing from the cracks. Up there on a high branch, tauntingly dangling its booty, this jackfruit had tempted many onlookers into evil thoughts of theft.

How gloriously ripe and ready to be devoured it looked now! Biju had cradled the fallen fruit like a baby and rushed in to gather members of the household who were readying themselves for a post-lunch nap. They were as ecstatic as Biju when they saw it. Biju placed the fruit on the dining table, over a clean cloth, others gathered around and admired the fruit as if it were a retrieved treasure.

"Let Binodini serve us," mother-in-law ordered.

Binodini froze. Was she to autopsy this fruit of audacious pungency that made her stomach roil? How could she possibly piece apart its impossibly sticky flesh and serve it to everyone present? Binodini didn't outrightly disobey. However, her face was contorted in vile repulsion, her nose was crinkled with held-up breath, and her lips were pursed into a thin line of evident distaste. Binodini could barely stand the fruity stench that clung to her saree and skin with the tenacity of a hungry wailing infant. Her in-laws were miffed and grumbled their disapproval. So thick was the air with friction and fragrance, that it could be knifed!

Sensing the tension about to explode, Biju hurried over to the jackfruit, his hands slick and thick with mustard oil and grabbed the fruit with firm hands and took to parsing it deftly. Binodini stood by Biju kaka's side, relieved, pinching her nose shut with a pincer grasp. Biju's calloused hands, wrinkled with experience, dexterously maneuvered the large knife and swiftly peeled away the fruit's prickly hide and pieced apart its sticky yellow mass. Soft, gluey, canary-yellow fruit-flesh glistened over his palm and fingers like coagulated sunlight. By the time Biju was done, Binodini had laid out fruit forks and delicate dessert bowls of bone-china with golden rim. Biju put the fruit pieces into the bowls, taking care not to smudge the serving dishes with his soiled fingers.

Binodini somehow managed to serve this offering to her in-laws suppressing her reflex to throw up. Tad appeased, they excused her at last. Biju fetched his crooked bowl from the kitchen and ate with his bare hands. He swore that the fruit tasted sweeter this way. The fruit indeed was ambrosial, Binodini's in-laws concurred. After all, it was conceived of the labor of love. Binodini's father-in-law had nursed the jackfruit sapling into its robust youth with great devotion. Biju had obsessively guarded the fruits against the pilferers in fruiting season. Though every night the lanky old watchman pedaled his rickety cycle through the neighborhood pouring his raspy breath into a metal pea whistle, Biju would sleep out in the front yard on a jute cot under the starlit sky, personally ensuring the safety the garden's bounty.

Biju's labor had paid off, his masters were happy, and his position seemed safe. The front porch was engorged with hot air, the crispness of which began to exorcise the sickening ripe jackfruit's smell lodged within Binodini's alveoli. She had always been sensitive to scents, particularly of ripe fruits - papaya, mango, banana, custard apple, the whole lot! At her father's, she was never made to suffer, and no one slighted her sensitivity. But she is not at her father's. Her eyes welled up with a surfeit of pain and spilt over like puddles in the rain.

Wiping away her tears, Binodini regarded the bonsai trees neatly lined in front of her. How dwarf they were, pretty little unnatural things! There was the Ficus tree with its impressive aerial roots, and the Jade plant with succulent oval green leaves and soft red-brown bark. Small white flowers and dark berries adorned the Fukien tea plant, while the Hawaiian umbrella tree fanned out its glossy dark green leaves in thick luxury. It repulsed her now though it had fascinated her in the beginning, the making of a bonsai tree—this methodical shrinking of life, forcing it into tight containers, this business of controlled oppression.

Binodini could feel the arrest in their slender stems, the constriction in their little leaves, which mirrored her spasms. The process was similar and had to start young: pick a small sapling from the right nursery/ choose a timid girl of sixteen of humble bearings. Make the casting rigid: plant the sapling in a bonsai pot, use wires, add enough soil to bury the roots /tie the girl to your boy, keep her in your house, and admonish until her silliness stops surfacing. Control the growth: manage the plant by pruning, wiring and re-potting/hem in the bride by disciplining, restricting and have her relearn everything the in-law's ways. Be vigilant. Repeat the last step as often as needed. Congratulations, you have a pretty Bonsai tree/a beautiful daughter-in-law—an abomination to behold!

Glossary

*Bodhu baran: The bride welcoming ceremony; the new bride receives gifts and blessings and is welcomed into the groom's family

*Doordarshan: An autonomous Government of India founded public service broadcaster

*Kailasha: A range of mountains of religious significance for the Hindus where they believe the main Hindu diety Shiva lives.

*Pallu: The loose end of a sari, worn over one shoulder or the head.

*Shiva: One of the main deities of Hinduism, whom Shaivites worship as the supreme god.

Eternal Garden

By Anushka Somavanshi

I t was a beautiful day. The sky was a brilliant shade of blue, the air was just the right amount of chilly and the Manor looked picturesque against such a stunning backdrop with its pink tinted brown stone framed by the golden sun rays. I could even hear the god-damned birds singing. The brightness of the day clashed painfully with the dark turmoil in my heart.

Now, I am hardly the kind of man who dwells too much on his emotions or feelings but lately things have changed. Some for the better, some for worse. Much, much worse. I've become acutely aware of my surroundings these days. Nothing escapes my notice. All my senses have been heightened. Perhaps, it's paranoia or perhaps something far more sinister. Under different conditions, I would have been able to relish the beauty of the manor's garden with greater appreciation. I notice all the colors of the flowers, the butterflies, trees, shrubs, everything.

But frankly, I'm sick of it. I'm mostly tired of smelling the godforsaken flowers everywhere I go. I could try disappearing to the darkest, dampest, most isolated corner of the manor and I'd somehow still smell them. My head hurt. I drank more, and faster to distract myself from that smell but it only became more sharper by the day. I'm not the sort of man who wastes his time on feminine employments like gardening. That was what my wife, Mrs. Wilfred Perrault, spent all her day doing.

Bloody waste of time, I always told her. She'd tend to her precious flowerbeds with so much focus and devotion you'd think she's running a professional business. She always came in the house smelling like the flowers she was with. Day in and day out, she would be at work in the garden with her little tools. So, I did her a favor, really. Burying her where she spent half her lifetime. I even buried the spade I hit her head with in the grave. Wasted a perfectly good spade but the blood wouldn't completely wash off of it. So, I did the only logical thing and tossed it in with my wife's body. I cannot ascertain the moment, or the spot, or the day when I decided that my life would be indisputably happier without the presence of my wife. It was simply an idle thought that took root in my mind years ago. Honestly, I never considered bringing those ideas to action. But one day when we were alone in her garden, I felt as though the moment was too perfect to pass up. She was facing away from me when I struck her with the first blow. It made a sickening crunch. However, my wife did not go down easily. She had a lot of fight in her.

I remember how she had turned back to face her attacker. The flicker of recognition and betrayal in her eyes had only served to enrage me further. I served blow after blow to her head, some landing on her face, until finally, she had stopped moving. That should've been the end of it but, it wasn't. All the imbeciles in my household staff had started asking endless questions about when their darling Mrs. Perrault would return home from her 'trip'. I had to fire them. I had no choice. Surely one can see how I was forced to.

For the first time in two decades, I was alone. Completely and utterly alone. I should be happy. No, no, I am happy. I have no one to interrupt me while I have my brandy or smoke my cigars. This is what I wanted. But I also wanted the bloody flowery smells to stop wafting into my house. I expected the flowers to die, of course. No one watering them or doing whatever my wife did all day. They should have died with her. But they persisted in their survival as if simply to spite me. My wife's revenge from the grave. I know that's ridiculous but I cannot trust my mind nowadays. It seems to be slipping farther and farther away from me. I go from being in a daze to being abruptly sensorily assaulted by all the lights, smells and sounds around me. The smells, most of all. That fragrant aroma which reminds me of her and that garden that won't let anything die in it. With the exception of my wife, of course.

I remember her telling me once, "This is a place full of life and death, Wilfred. It's natural.... It's a cycle. Everything breaks down and rises back up, again and again. Once these plants die, they leave behind seeds for new life to emerge. So do humans in a way. Like these flowers. The beauty lies in the mortality."

Unlike the mysterious garden, the manor had fallen into disrepair. Thick sheets of dust covered the furniture, the windows, all of it. I meant to hire a new household staff. I did. But I had to get rid of that smell first. I knew that as soon as someone stepped in this house they would be overwhelmed by the fragrance. They would ask questions! They would walk into the garden and dig up her grave. They would know! Somehow, they would know! I was certain of this. No! I simply cannot let that happen. Just because she had lost her life did not mean I had to, as well. I had to save myself. From her...or from that garden. I am not certain of where the real evil lay but they had to be connected. It's impossible to determine how this idea entered my mind but once it did, it refused to go. I could suffer no more!

You must know I am not a madman. I am calm and rational. I know what I must do next. The garden must go. The flowers must go. The fragrance must go. I grabbed an old, leathery gardening shear with the intention of tearing down every plant, shrub, flower I could see. As long as the garden lived, the decaying specter of my wife would continue to live in it. I could not escape her fragrance no matter where I went so naturally, I had to desecrate all remaining reminders of her existence. I was a man with a plan. If she continued to torment me with these smells, I would personally put an end to it. But no! That is madness. It cannot be possible for her to torture me beyond the grave. She was gone! I was free! But I felt more imprisoned by her than ever before. She would not let me go! I was bound to her by that bloody garden! I had begun screaming at the sky when I reached the garden, or perhaps I was already screaming before that. It is impossible for me to say. I did not even know if I was screaming in pleasure, agony or anguish! All I knew was that I had to wreck this place until it was unrecognizable. My screams intensified when I realized I couldn't cut the plants before me! I checked the shears' blades myself and they were so sharp I drew blood from my thumb. In my desperation, I started uprooting the plants with my hands but they wouldn't budge from the soil! I cried and cried! I cursed myself and the moment I killed my wife. I knew now that my fate had been sealed the moment, I bludgeoned my wife's pretty skull with a spade. I was on a track to death from that moment, everything was inevitable. While I lay there in the shrubbery, wailing with despair, the fragrance grew sharper in my nose. I knew it was her before I turned back. The knowledge of her presence did nothing to prepare me to face her. When I saw her, the blood in my body went cold like ice. She did nothing to hide her face or what I had done to it. It was still bruised and bloody from my attack but weeks of rotting in the soil had given it a grey-green mottling look with brown blooms of decay.

The skin from the right side of her face and head was hanging in ragged strips of flesh that was crusted with dried blood, gaping open to reveal the skull beneath. Her eyes were burning pits of hatred and they looked straight at me. Despite her ghastly death-like appearance, she smelled like blooming flowers. I remained kneeling in the same position, paralyzed, as she drew closer and whispered secrets in my ears that only a dead woman would know. I felt her cold, stony fingers lock themselves around my throat and raise me above the ground with a strength I did not know she possessed. I choked and struggled for breath, all in vain! Then suddenly everything went dark. The last thought in my head was of gratitude that I never had to smell that fragrance again.

The Scent of Kindness

By Vishaal Pathak

My best times are outside. Sunshine, sprinklers, a walk around the park, chasing away the birds, rolling in the grass sometimes when my back feels itchy and no one's looking. Almost always that's also when they all start looking. Except Jerry. But he can tell. Jerry hates the smell of grass on my skin. More than I hate baths that he almost always has to give me if he sniffs it on me. Or the nice lady who pretends she's all nice but clips my nails and distracts me to look somewhere else while she jabs my skin with some sort of shot that's supposed to protect me. I fall for that trick every time.

But she gives me a treat the next instant without fail so I try and not make a big deal about it. Last time around she took Jerry in the corner and whispered with concern, albeit hesitatingly. Now, I couldn't hear what she said – not that it would've made a difference – but I know what it was all about. I very well do. Jerry has since been a little off. I see it, I can sense it, but most importantly, I can smell it on him. I have that power. Back in my days, I helped crack many a case. We did it together – me and Jerry. In fact, we go a long way back. We graduated top of the class – both of us – at our respective schools and were recruited by the academy right off the bat. Legend has it that they were waiting in the parking lot during our convocation and rushed with offers as soon as we got off stage.

The two of us were teamed up to solve some of the most challenging cases on our side of the city. They called us J&T. For the 10 years that J&T were in service, our block was the most peaceful not just in the city but the whole province. Nobody could steal or defraud or harm another under our nose. Not one case went unsolved. No sir, not under our watch. And then, the inevitable happened. We were both relieved with dignity and we both moved to the suburbs in search of a more peaceful life. It made sense that we stuck together, missing one of it each.

"Terry. Terrrrry!" He'd call out. Would no longer beat the drums on my ear.

The nice lady said of my late Uncle Tim who went through a similar episode that a reconstructive surgery wouldn't help since being in such proximity to a noise of such intensity virtually shreds the insides of the ear to pieces. Uncle Tim had to go to a care home. I am fortunate I spend my time with Jerry at least. But that's not the only thing I want him to fill his day with. He fills my bowl with M&M's and special treats, takes me walking to the park and throws the frisbee around for me to catch and bring it back to him, he gives me baths I hate an awful lot, but soon that's all set to change, and he will need something else – someone else to fill his heart with. I've been sniffing for ages and I can tell immediately which one of you – no offence intended – have the worst of intentions. You could slice open a lemon, mix some old porridge, some nasty disease and an awful lot of treats into a bag and I would still pick whatever it is that the job at hand needs me to. The job at hand – the one I've assigned myself – is to find Jerry a soulmate.

'You could make a mistake too,' you'd say. I sure could, only I never do. I did it for a living, I do it for my life, after all. I've been unlucky, but only the one unfortunate time – and for that, I've spent many nights crying. The nice lady must've said I was inconsolable, because Jerry spent the next few nights cradling me in my bed. Friends from the services sent me an awful lot of toys to soothe my anxiety. I get nightmares even now sometimes, and I don't know how Jerry can sense it, but he does so every single time. He wakes me up gently and stays right beside until I've fallen asleep again.

'How to smell kindness on someone?' you'd ask. I could tell you, but what would that leave for us folk to do? I'm trained. Experienced. And also gifted. So, rest assured, understand that he's in good hands – for now. I just want to pass on that baton to someone kind and wonderful. And bring together a union that will value and cherish each other for the rest of their lives. Hopefully this time around, it will be forever.

'But give us something.' Okay. I will. For you folks won't stop pestering me. I met Jerry when he was only 21. I had sniffed many humans until then, but Jerry was different; he smelled differently too. He was kinder than anyone else I'd seen. Often, he'd put himself the last. For him, the city, public safety and even I came before. When Jerry fell in love five summers ago with Tanya, she moved in with him. Jerry was the happiest I'd ever seen him. Her fragrance was different too. Like a breath of fresh air. She'd bring me treats sometimes, gave me an awful lot of belly rubs.

The three of us were practically family. When free, we'd drive around in the car, watching sunsets or going to one of those drive-in theatres where you could park your car and watch movies. So, it hurt me a lot when, about two summers ago, I began to smell something alarming on her. I don't know what it was but I had to caution them. I woofed and woofed until they took it seriously and took her to her nice lady. It turned out something serious. In no time, she was gone. We both lost our spirits. Work kept getting harder and harder. We were both sad and anxious. And just when things seemed as if they'd get back on track, the inevitable happened. We got a call one day about a hostage situation.

On any other day, it would've been just something we were prepared to handle. But that day, even with the best of our intentions, and the best of our training, and the best of the equipment, we erred – albeit only slightly – but it cost us a lot. Don't get me wrong. We saved everyone. But we were a second too late – I was too late – to sniff out an explosive placed at the far end of the parking lot behind the building. It went off right in my face. Jerry was sent flying several feet in the air. And that, marked the end of our glorious years in peacekeeping. We moved to the suburbs because it doesn't remind us of the city, our jobs and most importantly, Tanya. But you can't live life in hiding. At some point, you have to tell yourself, it was not your fault. If it was – you must forgive yourself. We're all flawed; there's only so much we can do.

'But why the urgency to find him someone?' you may question. Well, you see, a cat has nine lives, but not our kinds. I also don't know the truth about a dog year equalling many human years, but my time here –

whether I like it or not – will be up soon. I have smelled on me what I smelled on Tanya. It is undeniable.

I am getting old and rusty too. The only good I still have intact is my superpower. Ah, it's time to go out again. Jerry just patted my back. Time for our evening walk, let me grab our frisbee. The way to the park is clean, but why take chances? I sniff all the way so we evade anything that could be an irritant or potentially harmful. Jerry walks right behind me. Time for work! I scan the park for potential matches. Must love dogs; cats are fine too.

Every time Jerry throws the frisbee a little further away, I take it to a stranger and make the face so they have to pet me. When they put their hand on my head, and run it down my fur, that's how I know. I catch a whiff. That's enough time for my judgement. I've now been doing it for a whole summer now, so I should find out soon if one exists in this park. Ah, there's one on that bench under the tree. She looks kind. Knitting a dog sweater. I shall take the frisbee to her. She likes my innocent eyes. I can tell because she touched her heart and is now petting me. Yes, go on. Go on.

"JERRRRRRRY!" I'd yell if I could. Oh, I might roll in the grass and won't mind having a bath later. Let me run back to him for now. Oh, come one Jerry. I found the one. I found the one. Yes, I am excited an awful lot. Yes, grab the walking stick and come on after. I shall be your eyes. Let's go Jerry, I can't calm down! Not today!

Aromatic Discoveries

By Iravati Kamat

E veryone who knew Varun would tell you that Varun was a people person. Of course, Varun would deny that. What does being a people person even mean!

Varun didn't feel he was particularly the most likable person in the room or that all the people he knew absolutely loved his company. What he would never deny, however, was that he couldn't survive without his tightly woven cocoon of friends and family.

Varun was used to arranging get-togethers at his house with his school friends, college friends and relatives. You name a group of dear ones and Varun could not wait to catch up with them, hang out and relive old memories. Even at work, he couldn't wait to chat with his colleague-turned-friends during breaks because it would boost his energy for the rest of the workday.

As for his family, he would gladly admit that they were his biggest strength. Starting from waking up to a bustling house to those lazy post-dinner chats, he wouldn't trade it for anything in the world. That's why today morning was quite special. Varun had returned from a work trip of about two days, something that could not be avoided even during the growing pandemic. He knew he had to isolate himself but he couldn't help but appreciate this moment. His room had a great view of the house, both kitchen and living room being in his line of sight. He sat in the far corner of his room, soaking in the familiar environment outside.

One hand held the mask that he had just taken off and the other hand was clutching a hot cup of tea, raveling the familiar taste. A few feet away he could see his grandmother sitting on a short but spacious and soft cushioned chair completely lost in her book, clutching her own cup of tea. He loved to observe her during such quiet moments. Mostly because he didn't have that privilege often as he would usually be on his way to work at this time. He loved this small, standstill moment of serenity his grandmother used to keep for herself after her morning prayer.

He could see his younger brother sitting or rather, lying on the sofa, not very far from their grandmother. The book he was supposed to be studying from laid forgotten on his lap, his hand furiously typing on his phone, his face adorning a very small smile. Something told Varun that that smile was worth investigating. After a few days when he would be free to roam around the house, he assured himself. His brother didn't have his own cup of tea but there was no suspense as to why that was the case. An acceptable amount of time post everyone's tea but still an hour or two before lunch, he would approach their mother to butter her up for a 'perfect' cup of coffee that only she could make. It wouldn't take long to convince her as usual because the coffee would help as he 'studied' the 'whole day' for his exams which were due in three weeks.

Sitting at the dining table in the kitchen was his sister, with his mother standing just behind her, meticulously working on her hair. Everyone in the house knew that his sister was old enough to be able to braid her own hair and that his mother always had more than a few tasks at hand to take out this time for that. But they always did it together anyway, taking time out for braiding the hair and chatting throughout it. All in the pretext of mixing the correct amount of aloe vera with oil, which his sister insisted was quite tricky, while his mother often said that it was not all that difficult. All in all, everyone knew not to interrupt them during this time.

As Varun was taking in the small details of the scene in front of him, his phone buzzed and although he was expecting a call about the results of the precautionary COVID-19 test, he was still startled. Carefully, setting the tea aside, he answered the phone and that was the moment his world tipped on its side. One moment he was sitting there, taking in everything around him and the next moment he was still sitting there staring at the closed door. A few medicines, clothes, masks, and a sanitizer sitting on the table in front of him were the only tells of what had transpired in that one moment. He sat there feeling slightly helpless with the closed door taunting him, taking away his only comfort that he was relishing in so peacefully a few moments ago.

While it was difficult to miss that he was living in a world eclipsed by a pandemic, his bubble of happiness had never let it get to him. He couldn't believe he had tested positive. There was hardly any fever or any other symptoms for that matter. He had hardly coughed a handful of times since morning.

Symptoms... Covid... Positive... His eyes immediately

went to the unfinished cup of tea that still sat there neglected. He almost launched himself at the tea picking it up with both his hands trying to feel the lingering traces of the warmth and bliss he had felt a few moments back. Varun finally brought the cup close to him and inhaled with as much force as he could gather, afraid of the outcome. Then it reached him, the faint fragrance of ginger and lemongrass, grounding him in that moment. He could do this. He was at his home, among loved ones, with only minor symptoms of the notorious Covid-19, isolated only for next 14 days, in a golden era of electronic wizardry. He could do this.

It was difficult. As much as digital communication with friends came to the rescue, it was not the same. He hadn't realized before how much physical presence of the people around him really mattered to him, how much of his happiness and energy came from the people around him. Maybe he was a people person. Huh, who knew!

Initially, he had thought his family just being on the other side of a thin wall would be his main source of comfort. He was looking forward to hearing the hustle and bustle in the living room, shouted name calls, and mundane discussions throughout the day. But the voices and noises had quieted down significantly compared to the usual liveliness of the house.

Apparently, COVID-19 had not affected just him in the house. But as everyone continued to go about their routine, it gave him the much-needed sense of normalcy. And even with quieted decibel levels and hushed tones outside his door, he knew that his family was trying to stick to their routine, maybe for his sake. So, he appreciated that as much as he appreciated the source of this information - the fragrance of the house. Another one of his brilliant little discoveries while he was isolated. It took some time to register it and relate it to the happenings on the other side of the door at first. But soon, within a day or two, his days were aligned with those happenings. His days used to start with the soothing sandalwood incense of agarbatti from his grandmother's morning puja and ended with the smell of haldi mixing with freshly boiled doodh for everyone to have it before sleeping.

It was not long before it felt like he was standing at the door basking in the aroma of the scene that was abruptly snatched away from. After taking bath, as he would open his laptop for work wondering what might be happening on the other side of the door, the aroma of the tea boiling at a distance mixed with a little bit of soothing fragrance of oil mixed with aloe Vera would reach him. Around the time he would finish his tea, dropped off at the door by someone, the aroma of freshly brewed coffee would fill the air and a smile would form on his face unmistakably.

Varun had never been more thankful for the air around him even though he needed his lungs full of it to live on a daily basis. He was even more thankful that closed doors did nothing to stop the airflow. He couldn't wait to share this little discovery with his family. He couldn't wait to tell his family they helped him much more than they thought, unknowingly. He knew that they would be glad to hear it if the silence on the other side of the door was anything to go by. Soon. His quarantine was ending soon.

On the 15th day, he was tested again. He could see his family hovering outside the door but at a distance. Soon. He was ready to put an end to this, feeling positive about testing negative. He couldn't wait for the next day to come.

The next day, the test results reached him first. Wanting to surprise his family, Varun peeked out of the room without particularly announcing it and he saw his grandmother stealthily putting a small agarbatti holder near his room before moving away without noticing him at all. The little discoveries didn't seem to cease.

Fragrances fade, Memories don't!

By Vibhuti Bhandarkar

One warm afternoon of my summer holidays, Nanma and I were at the sun-bathed front porch of our brightly painted farmhouse in the sleepy Karmirem countryside. Sitting there at my grandmother's feet always had a calming effect on me. I was ready to dose off as Nanma's fingers massaged my head in a soothing rhythm. The coconut oil liberally poured on the top of my head, trickled down behind my ears and I loved the tickling sensation. Its sweet fragrance, a treat for my senses.

I could feel my eye-lids grow heavy, and I'm sure they looked like the shutters on Uncle Patrick's liquor shop threatening to come down any minute. The intermittent shrill cries of the sea-gulls in the distance was the only sound that broke through the quiet and kept me from drifting off for some time. Eventually, I had dozed off with my head in the hammock of Nanma's lap. It wouldn't be an exaggeration if I'd told you that everybody around- young and old, would come visiting my grandmother for one reason or another. Our septuagenarian sitting in her rocking chair was like the grandmother to the entire fishing hamlet. They had begun calling her 'Nanma' long before I had come into existence. While I was snoozing Celina must have brought Nanma a plate of freshly prepared Jackfruit chips.

"Ghare karo!" Nanma had squealed, unable to conceal her love for the fried delicacy, stirring me from my nap.

As I peeled my eyes open, I saw the beautiful Celina being welcomed into Nanma's warm embrace. "So true to your name you are! Seh-LEEN-ah, a vision of heaven itself," Nanma chortled, nibbling at the treat "Dev borre korum!"

"Thank you? Nanma, did you just thank me? These jackfruit chips simply turn you into a totally different person, men!" Poking fun at the food-lover, Celina grinned, and I chuckled.

"Hello there, Teensy," Celina smiled down at me. Nobody called me Tina at Nanma's place. They all had different nicknames for me, but that Celina should have a pet name for me, felt very endearing. As she bent over to plant a delicate peck on my forehead, I caught a whiff of the beautiful fragrance of Jasmines from her clothes. As I peered into Celina's eyes, I saw that they were as blue as the crystal-clear waters of the sea.

I was thirteen years old by then, and I remember I was becoming increasingly enamored by the glamorous faces on the silver screen in those days. However, that moment onwards, Celina's flawless face became the only one I longed to see, sans make-up, yet so stunning.

'I wonder how she smells so divine, when the entire area reeks of dried fish,' I'd said to myself. All the ladies in the house used to gossip about our neighbor Solomon's daughter, Celina.

"God only knows men, how that ugly fisherman got such a beautiful daughter!" All my elder cousins would excitedly whisper when Celina came visiting, either to borrow something from the kitchen, or bringing basketful of fresh catch that Solomon sent. I never went running with them from one part of the house to another, just to get a glimpse of her.

"Solomon always sends me big-big White Pomfrets," Nanma would gush in gratitude.

My mother had ventured to order Celina, "Can you get us those shucked Oysters the next time?"

"Kidde, khaje ge tain?" Nanma had wittily snubbed my mother, by asking her if she thought harvesting Oysters was as easy as snacking. Vacations at Nanma's farmhouse were short and far apart, so there had hardly ever been any chance for me to befriend Celina.

On the few occasions that I had crossed paths with Celina in the past, maybe at the market or on Sundays at Church, she had always thrown kind smiles towards me whenever our eyes met. Even though I'd always meant to, I had never really managed to respond with the same warmth.

That afternoon however, Celina was standing so close to me. And I had the strongest urge to strike a conversation with her but again, all I could do was stare!

"Nanma, are you going to make all her hair grow in one day only? Why have you poured so much coconut oil, I can smell it till here!" Celina teased.

"Tchah! What to do? Just look at her, na! Who will say she's a girl? Call her Tom, not Tina," Nanma grunted.

"Aavois!" Celina exclaimed, looking slightly annoyed, but had refrained from scolding Nanma.

"Come on, Teensy! Tu hedpakk yetta?" An invitation from Celina to loiter around with her was too tempting to pass, even for an introvert like me! She put her palm out and clasped mine. Hand in hand, we headed for the beach. That day and the next, and all the remaining days of my summer holidays that year, I went tagging along with Celina wherever she'd take me like her pet puppy.

Once back home in Bombay, I wrote her a long letter during the Diwali holidays, telling her how I would not be able to visit Nanma until the next summer holidays, and how I would miss her company, terribly.

Even as I wrote I felt a pang of hurt lodge in my heart. I could feel a constriction in my throat. Tears welled up, but I didn't let them fall lest they should blot the ink on the paper. I wrote,

Fragrances,
That I brought home,
From your touch,
Left me breathless,
Haunted me much.
Fragrances,
That I fear are,
Faster than memories fading,
Leaving me lost and lonely,
In salty tears, wading!

She had replied with an equally sweet letter, no poetry, but everything written in a neat hand. Once, twice, but my third letter had had no reply.

I switched to calling her every weekend. As soon as my forefinger began dialing her number in the rotary of the big black telephone, my heart would start thumping so loudly that I was almost unable to hear the ring go through. Her melodious voice would come to my ears through the receiver, and I would forget all that I had planned to say. Just listening to Celina's stories was like the fuel that kept me going through the subsequent week at school. I spent most part of my classes daydreaming of strolling and lolling on the beach all day with Celina. Eventually, the phone calls between us dwindled too for she was mostly always away from her home, and her folks forgot to remind her to call me by the time she got back.

Meanwhile, Celina's accomplishments as the most graceful dancer in Karmirem came as tidbits of news. Celina had become the topic of juicy gossip over long phone calls between my mother and Nanma.

"Nanma says, she's Ujjo! Fire on the dance floor," mother told me. Word was that she had joined her cousin, Russel D'Souza's dance troupe. The day she had stepped in, the troupe had immediately been signed up for a year's contract to dance at the 'Live Goan Cultural Shows' aboard Panjim's most famous 'The Dona Paula' Cruise. By December, Celina had thus become quite a legend in the village, and a lucky charm of sorts for Russel's troupe.

"Solomon has given me New Year's special passes to the show, FREE!" Nanma's voice had screeched in excitement, through the handset. So, we began packing at Nanma's behest, and I was overjoyed with the sudden change of plans.

"It is going to be the best Christmas ever," I shouted, and danced around as my family settled down at the dining table in the center of Nanma's kitchen. I was giggling, uncontrollably!

"Makka kalna!" Nanma raised her eyebrows at me.

"What are you not understanding?" I laughed.

"Kitte ithle khitkhitto go tukka?" Nanma demanded to know what was causing so much mirth.

I realized I was acting like a giddy-headed teenager in love! Now, I couldn't possibly tell Nanma why, could I?

But Christmas passed us by, without any sign of Celina. Uncle Patrick had come shoddily dressed as Santa, handing out colorfully wrapped gifts to us like we were still a bunch of naive children. I was unable to see the fun in it, anymore!

'How could Celina not come to visit us at Christmas?' I did not cry out loud. I sulked in corners. 'The Dona Paula' Cruise was my only hope. I kissed the tickets and put them carefully in the drawer by my bedside. The glorious day finally arrived which promised to close the year on a happy note. An absolutely grand evening aboard the cruise in Panjim, began to unfold. When I finally saw Celina step foot on stage, I was already imagining us standing together, my palm clasped in hers during the count down into the New Year. She would kiss my cheeks, and I would hug her tight, while watching the fireworks in the night sky. I was startled out of my reverie, as the peppy music began and Russel's troupe began their performance of the Corridinho- a traditional Portuguese folk-dance form. It was an energetic dance performed in pairs. The girls formed the inner whorl while the boys formed the outer circle. The two circles rotated, while the pairs also revolved. At a certain moment when the music jumped to a stronger beat, the dancers hit their feet to the floor with more intensity while dancing. In one dance routine, the music was at a slower tempo, the dancers paired up and embraced, while doing the Waltz, spinning at their appointed spots on stage.

Although, Celina had danced like any other Corridinho dancer in her troupe, choreographed to perfection, she did appear superlatively graceful and attractive than the rest. One flick of her kerchief as she stepped into the front row while flawlessly executing the dance moves, and she had received a thunderous applause. After the show, she was singled out and showered praise upon, by locals, by Indian tourists, and foreigners as well. Mother and I had gone to meet her outside their green room. I was sure she'd be thrilled to see me.

"What a pleasant surprise!" Celina had squealed when she spotted me waving at her. She weaved her way through the people milling about the deck, and rushed towards us. She pecked my cheek and I hugged her tight, but something was sorely amiss. Her lips were moving, talking to my mother, and one arm still hugged me around my waist, but her blue eyes were darting about, as if searching for someone.

"Celina, I..." She didn't hear me squeak. I watched the artificially curled black locks dance at her nape, while she chatted with my mother, animatedly. I was desperately waiting to get her attention.

"Why did you stop calling me?" I had asked, but my words had fallen short of her ears. Just then it struck me, what had been niggling at the back of my mind!

'What's that smell of some cheap perfume? Why doesn't she smell like Jasmines anymore?' I remember thinking to myself. As I stood there, pinned to her side, she had put her free hand out and grabbed at a man's sleeve, pulling him closer to our trio.

"Russel D'Souza," Celina had introduced the man in a garishly dramatic manner.

'Why is she blushing so much? He has her undivided attention!' The smell of cheap cologne had got stronger, as he came to stand by her side.

"Celina, don't you love me?" I had asked, trembling from top to toe. She turned to look at me, blankly. I don't think she'd heard me over the sound of his loud booming voice and other noises around us.

"Teensy!" Celina had smiled at me, and planted a delicate peck on my forehead, but this time I caught a whiff of a very different scent.

The scent of betrayal!

The Fragrance Gift

By Amal Behbehani

Mama told me that if a person gets you a perfume for your birthday, it is a sign that you got to wash more often. And I've been getting perfume box sets on my birthday ever since I was eight.

And no matter how many times I shower and scrub myself, I still find a new set at my birthday the following year, amongst the pile of gifts. I can't even tell if it is that obvious; if people turn their nose or hold their breath when I chat with them. You can't chew and hold your breath at the same time, can you? Then my lunch buddies find me fine. At least Pumba knew from when the animals at the watering hole fainted at his presence. I don't have any sign that lets me know if I smell. I can't recognize my scent, and I have taken steps to play less sports or any activity that leads me to sweat. I take the elevator at every mall, and excuse myself from physical education at school. I miss playing soccer, but a good scent is better than having fun.

My family and extended relatives don't help. They smile at me, and laugh with me, but then for souvenirs I get soap bars and oils. I came outright and asked my cousin once, but she laughed at my concern and said I had nothing to worry about. When the stray cats started to follow me home, that's when I decided something needs to change. A trip to the mall to find a new perfume results in mama chatting with her friends, buying her own perfume, and then grabbing any random item for me to use. What fragrance she chose had strawberry, which I'm allergic to. I had to stay home for a few days, dreaming of strawberries with stick legs chasing me down.

The next time, I went with Baba to the store. Baba sat outside, reading the newspaper, as I glanced through the perfume counter. All seemed expensive for what is basically water with a scent. One promised to be what royalty use, and the other what is named after the sheikh. When I asked the shop staff which royalty used the perfume, he looked on blankly, and laughed when I asked if the sheikh knew his name was used for the perfume. In the end I decided on one shaped as a teddy bear. People loved teddy bears, right? They like to cuddle the toy. It gave me hope that this would change my scent. I used it for a week, and though it did seem to change my scent, my cheeks hurt from all the pinches the aunts and uncles gave it, treating me like a child. I handed the teddy bear perfume to my younger cousin.

I asked my sister if I can use one of her perfumes. She was on the phone, and just nodded and waved me off as I took one. I sprayed it several times, over my shoulder and on my face – granting a few minutes of coughing up what might have been my lung. I skipped down the school's hallway, confident that this perfume would work. My sister was popular in her class, and if she liked something, everyone liked it. Taking a seat in the back, I start to pull out my books from bag. The girl next to me coughs, and wrinkles her nose, but doesn't say anything else. The boys, however, cough out loud and yell across the room asking who doused themselves with perfume. I sat lower in my seat, not creating eye contact with anyone.

"This is oud fragrance, Yuma. Why the hell did you spray it all over you? One dose is enough for the whole day." My sister told me as she held my backpack, with an obvious attempt at trying not to laugh at my face. She made me walk outside for a while to roll the fragrance off before pushing me into the shower. I didn't leave my room the next day.

Mama would have dragged me to school, but grandma told her to leave me be. Nana left my favorite snacks by the door, a plate of colorful tea cakes. Once I saw them, I tiptoed my way to her room, afraid someone else would spot me and push me to go to school. In nana's room, she sat on her bed cross-legged, watching her favorite TV show on the screen my dad brought for her room. She used to come and visit us once a week, but since she became old, she now lives here in the room that used to be Baba's home office. I take the plate to her and share my tea cakes with her, knowing mama would've lectured me about nana's sugar levels.

"Tell me, child, why are you hiding?" She asks, and I explain between tears and bites of the tea cake, about the perfume gifts and buying perfumes. She listened as she watches her TV show, patting my hand every few minutes. When the tea cakes are gone, she closes the TV and faces me.

"Child, you must know the truth: no cares what gift they give you. A birthday gift for kids is chosen randomly, what is on the shelf they could find the quickest. Now, if this was a gift from a boyfriend, or your wedding day, I would worry. But dear child, no one cares what you smell like, or even have the time to sniff you. Unless you are running outside for hours end or rolling over in the mud, the adults won't notice anything amiss. And even then, you are the child that takes the most baths in this household. You are constantly worried about your scent, when people won't even notice if you changed your clothes today." She pats my hand again.

"If it is not the gift from your parents, or your siblings, then a perfume set is just a perfume set. Be more confident of your own scent."

"But nana, you can say that because you can't smell anything." I whine.

"Oh, I can smell, I just choose not to." She winks. I frown.

"But mama said –"

She lightly smacks my head. "Listen to what I'm saying. No one cares what you smell like. Just don't pour Oud over your head." She then shows me how a true lady sprays perfume – she grabs her perfume, sprays it to the ceiling, then glides through it. She lets me try as well, wearing her pearls and heels, as she sprays me with her perfume.

"…and what are my two favorite girls are doing? Hmm? Skipping school?" Baba says from the doorway, leaning against the door with a smile on her face. He glances to the plate, and winks to nana.

"No more desserts for you today, mama." He joins us in our parade, letting nana spray the fragrance all over him as he turns around for her. The next day, I went to school, and did not spray oud or any perfume. My friends came over and said hello. My classmates talked to me during class. My teacher didn't wrinkle her nose when she handed me my papers. No one looked at me weirdly, or snickered about my smell. I kept waiting for it, but when the bell rang at the end of the day, no one came suggested or joked about my smell. I found myself walking home with my friends, asking me why I didn't show up yesterday.

"I had fun with nana." I smiled secretively. We end up going to my house, and spent the day trying out nana's perfumes, sneaking baklava to her room when mama wasn't looking. A few years later, I came across a whiff of the familiar fragrance while I was shopping with my friends. I went to the counter, and there it was, a small blue bottle, with the same scent of that day. I bought two of them, and placed them on my desk, unopened. I gave the second bottle for Baba's birthday, and saw the moment he recognized it when he unwrapped it. I kept my bottle for the hard days, for when I needed nana the most.

When I start to feel the thoughts swirling in my head again. It ebbed and flowed, jumping from worries of the fragrance I wore, to the friends I gained and lost, to my choice in pursuing education, to being rejected by the university I wanted, to the men who came for my hand in marriage, only because of family's last name.

Nana's room would be where mama would find me on those days, sitting on the bed. She would tell me it would get better and nudge my feet under the blanket. She did not mind that Baba and I didn't let anyone change Nana's room. The room was empty of her laughs, of her fragrance, of her smiles and stolen treats. But any time I sprayed that perfume, I would feel her presence besides me, reminding me to accept myself as I am.

Aroma Therapy

By Sneha Acharekar

Raima had just reached home. Physically. Her mind was still hovering at work around the organized desk that Ralph sat at. The few hours that she had spent at work that afternoon, kept playing in her thoughts. She had known him as an acquaintance and colleague for many years. However, it had been just about a month since they had become good friends after having started working on the same project. Ralph came across as one of the very few talented people that her workplace had recruited. He was calm, intelligent and dependable. She felt comfortable when he was around and work sailed smoothly when he worked with her. She had been playfully teasing him since a few days about him ageing and yet being single. She wanted to know more about him.

He had begun to teach her to drive the car, of late. It was her plan. This way she would get a chance to take in his therapeutic scent for another hour after work as he took the risk of letting her learn to drive, using his own car. She kept delaying the process of letting him know that he had been a great teacher by feigning that she was still a bad driver; hoping some day he would make some move!

Was he really single? He was never linked to anyone at work all these years. Raima always saw him with his group of guy friends when at work. She felt a severe coldness of disquiet creeping inside her. She had developed intense feelings for him over the last few weeks of having worked closely with him.

He had ordered a pizza for them at lunchtime. She let him order the pizza of his choice. She smiled at herself when he refused to accept her share of the expense. He liked her, but his feelings seemed so controlled. That Raima couldn't put a bridle on her feelings that seemed to be galloping towards him, was the issue.

"Your treat next time" Ralph said, unaware about the cantering effect of his words on her heartbeats.

It had been two hours since she was home but the effect of his presence around her for the whole day wasn't wearing out. She sat by the window with a hot cup of cardamom coffee that she made for herself. She realized only after the fourth sip that she had forgotten to add sugar to her coffee. She continued to stare into the cup and inhaling the scintillating aroma of her beverage. Her thoughts ran back to Ralph's way of making his own coffee at the vending machine. She continued to drink her sugarless coffee as she watched the rains drench everything outside. The air was fragrant with a mild petrichor rising slowly and steadily into a strong scent. Ralph's silhouette against the window near his desk flashed in her thoughts again. He had spent five long minutes staring at the heavy rain splashing on the shut window panes of their work cabin that afternoon while he continued to speak in a hushed manner into his cell phone.

"I find it difficult to digest that he is single." Raima had whispered into her own cell phone to Sharanya, her childhood friend.

"Stop thinking that way. May be he was dating someone a while ago... May be he's available at the moment. He does seem to like you, right?" Sharanya asked.

"How would I know?" Raima sulked.

"How can you not know, Raima? A woman almost always knows when a man is interested in taking their friendship to another level... He has complimented you so many times about your appearance, right? That's one of the signs. The way he looks at you, is another. The way he treats you, yet another. You're just not paying enough attention." Sharanya blurted.

Raima shook her head to put away that conversation with her friend from her mind and chose to drift back to thinking about the time spent with Ralph at work that afternoon. He had a headache before lunch and had made a suggestion about a head massage. Raima had embarrassingly told him she would have loved to help him with a head massage but didn't want the onlookers at work to brew up stories about them. He had smiled and told her that he had just made a comment and wasn't expecting any massage. She had kept her eyes on her computer screen hoping he hadn't noticed how the butterflies had fluttered inside her. There had been times when he had told her how dainty her nails looked when they were painted red. Or how he loved the way she shaded her eyelids. He had also urged her into an impromptu shopping trip last week.

But friends do that too. How would I know whether there's more to it? But do 'just friends' hold your hand and deeply inhale the scent of nail-paint from your fingers?

Raima's lips curled into a coy smile as the memory surfaced across her mind. As she took the last sip of her coffee and the drizzle outside turned into a heavy downpour, Raima picked up her phone and wondered hesitantly for a minute before she sent him a text: *Still at work?*

He responded after a few minutes: *Yes. Another half an hour.*

The evening soon switched off into a dark night. Raima could barely take him off her mind. She sat on her bed and stared at the walls of her bedroom as she kept running and rerunning through his thoughts. She had almost fallen asleep with her phone in her hands when it vibrated and the screen lit up his name. She woke up instantly and read his text.

"*Yes. Just reached home. Was out with friends.*"

It was a response to her previous text - "*Awake?*"

As Raima's heartbeats were about to normalize their pace, another message lit up her phone: "*Do me a favor?*"

With trembling fingers, Raima responded, "*Sure.*"

"*Tomorrow, bring along yourself to work with that red nail-paint.*"

***

The next morning, Raima walked into their work space with a glow of expectation on her face. Hopefully, today was the day. Perhaps, Ralph would express mutual feelings. Ralph turned around in his chair to face her as the whiff of her perfume announced her arrival.

"Good morning!" he smiled and raised his eyebrows in appreciation upon noticing a decked-up in a black dress, hair tied in a loose ponytail that flowed on her left shoulder and a luscious red on her lips and nails. "Wow, you look gorgeous!"

Raima smiled in an awkward manner, unable to acknowledge the compliment appropriately as Ralph continued, "Did you get it along?"

Raima lifted her hand and brought her fingers in front of his face to flaunt the red nail-paint on it. Ralph held her fingers in his and bent forward to take in the scent of the fresh coat of paint on her nails. Raima's heart skipped another beat.

"Ah! This is aroma-therapy!" Ralph exclaimed.

Raima chuckled and even as she felt elated, argued, "If you think this is aroma therapy, you should experience the scent of the flowers that have bloomed since last night on the tree right outside my house. The whole area is fragrant of them."

"Night jasmine?" Ralph asked.

"I thought of it as that too, but I was so mesmerized with them the whole evening, yesterday; I 'googled' and found out that it's called the 'Devil's tree'! The scent was so strong yet so smooth on the nerves. It's heavenly - like you don't need anything else if you can keep smelling it's aroma. I was obsessing over its fragrance until I read that it brings one bad luck."

"You don't believe that, do you?"

Raima shrugged. That would depend on what today has in store for me, she thought as he took another deep breath from her fragrant nails.

"Okay, don't tell anyone I asked for this. Where's the bottle?" Ralph's eyes twinkled.

Raima took a few seconds to process the question in her head, "Bottle?"

"This... nail-paint bottle" he leant closer and said softly

"I wanted to buy the same for someone special."

The smile vanished from Raima's face as she repeated the heart-wrenching words, "Someone special?"

"If I tell you about my relationship... How much can I trust you?" he looked at her and Raima noticed his cheeks turn pink.

Something inside her shattered into pieces. She was heartbroken and angry at the same time. In a fit of an inexplicable emotion, she ran off at the mouth, "I thought you were hitting on me all this while!"

Ralph took the comment as a joke and put it away, "Can I trust you?"

"What do you think? I am a Capricorn, too. May be you can trust me as much as you trust yourself?" Raima tried to smile but pulled her hand away from his.

"So, it's a more complicated case of 'it's complicated'. I don't know if you would just start getting judgmental about me. But... we were dating. It was a few years ago. Then we took a break." Ralph seemed hesitant to continue. "You won't tell anyone right? I hope I can trust you."

"If you have your doubts about that, don't tell me anything further. It's okay." Raima looked at Ralph in his eyes. A part of him seemed to be in a dilemma. Yet another part of him seemed to want to vent it out to her. "We took a break for a year and he drifted away during that time. We continued to remain in touch. I never got over him and... Neither did he." Ralph continued.

"She, you mean?" Raima asked pretending disinterest.

Ralph put up a sarcastic grin and looked into his computer. He continued to pretend to be working on the presentation that was open on his screen and spoke again, "He. Shishir. I like men."

This piece of information was completely unexpected and it hit Raima hard. She did not think an inkling before she repeated, "You like men!"

Realising how it had sounded when she had said that, she scoffed, "Listen, it's difficult enough to convince my parents to accept a son-in-law from another religion, please don't add the complication of your sexual preferences to it!"

***

"He thought I was joking! Damn, that Devil's tree. That is what brought in the bad luck." Raima complained as she whined away to Sharanya on the phone.

"Don't be stupid. Just spend some more time and make him aware about your feelings. Who knows he may change..."

"Sharanya, he likes men. Since years. How is that going to change? No wonder we've never seem him date any lady at work."

"Don't lose hope. Tomorrow, when he's teaching you to drive - just make a move."

"Bye, Sharanya. I wonder if you are even listening! The entire purpose of that driving class... Ugh! I know how to drive! Well... atleast I'm not gonna feel rejected by him." Raima squealed and disconnected the call.

She walked into her kitchen grumpily and made her evening tea. She crushed a small piece of ginger in the contents before placing the vessel on the flame and added a drop of lemon grass essence right when the tea boiled and bubbled up to the rim of the vessel. She strained the tea in her usual cup and added a dash of milk to it. She walked to her bedroom next, with her cup of tea.

The evening had blossomed outside her bedroom's window. She took in a deep breath and hurled silent curses at the Devil's tree. She shut her eyes for a few seconds, congregated the scattered emotions in her head and savored the fragrance. Ralph's scent started to fade from her mind. The scent of the flowers lingering in the air overpowered the scent of her lemon grass - ginger tea. A minute later, she opened her eyes and looked at the tree ladened with ochre-yellow flowers and broke into a smile as she took another deep breath of the clear evening, in.

Eau de Culpabilité

By Louisa Ellemind

F rances' eyes shot open and she listened to the soft click of the door closing in the frame. It was the first time she had been awoken by such a quiet noise, and it took her a moment to register what was happening.

She sat up in her bed, hung her stuffed kangaroo around her neck by its velcro hands and slowly approached her bedroom door. The stench coming from outside made her stop. She did recognize the smell. It was how she knew that her little brother had played with her toy car and had broken it. It was how she knew that her mother hadn't forgotten to buy her the toy drone she had promised her; she just didn't have the money. It was how she knew that her teacher hadn't been right to yell at her that time she was talking in class. It came in waves, and almost everybody carried it, except for babies. It smelled sweet and gentle when it was light, and that was what her dad had smelt like before tonight. It was bearable for Frances when it was moderate, similar to when one of the twins let out a loud one in the corner, and the whole class laughed. She had smelt hints of it in the City Centre, of it getting bad, getting terrifying, but she wasn't allowed to go off on her own, so she had just held onto her mum or dad's hand and the spook had passed quickly.

This was different. This was unlike anything she had experienced before. It wasn't a sound that had awoken her. This smell would have woken up a bear from hibernation. She could feel it take over her body. Where she should have felt tired, she felt the stench instead. Where she should have felt frightened, she felt the stench instead. Her bare feet that should have felt cold, they felt of stench instead. So, what on earth possessed her to open that door?

Perhaps she was curious, perhaps she wanted to warn her family, perhaps she no longer had possession of her wits, and the stench had taken over the movements of her body, too. Frances opened the door and took a step into the hall. She saw her father hang up his coat. He had a grin on his face and a spring in his step.

"Hey, monkey", he said when he saw her, "can't sleep?"

Frances shook her head and stared. The smell was getting worse. Her eyes were watering from it.

"It's the smell", she told him, "it woke me up."

He frowned. "I can't smell anything. Are you sure it wasn't a dream?"

Frances shook her head. "No dream", she said. Her father looked slightly concerned. He would spend part of the rest of the night googling his daughter's symptom of smelling things that weren't there. Her next olfactory hallucination, as he called them from then on, would lead him to take her to the doctor. The doctor would attribute it to stress because the little girl was, by that time, severely stressed.

"Where did you go?", she asked him now, "why weren't

you asleep?"

Dad laughed. "Kids don't tell their dads when to go to bed, dear. Why aren't you asleep?" He read her a story on the sofa, then tucked her into bed. All the while Frances kept staring at him. Because no matter where he went, the stench went with him. Frances couldn't sleep very well from then on. Whenever she heard the door click, she would reach for her bin to catch the sick that never came.

School became a break for her. The smells there made her curious, not terrified and gaggy, and if something threatened to get worse, she could just walk away or be able to flee after an hour. Even when he wasn't at home, part of the stench was still there, no matter how much she opened all the windows. Frances did her best to hide how much the smell impacted her. She figured that everyone must be able to smell it, but that she was the only one bothered by it because she was such a sensitive soul. Frances didn't want to be such a sensitive soul. She just wanted to be normal. Which was hard to be, even at school, even when the smells were fun and light. She had fallen asleep twice in class the week her teacher called in her parents. It was a mystery to them.

After the first time she had been caught sleeping in class, her parents had moved up her bedtime to 40 minutes earlier. After the second time, they had taken away her nightlight so that she couldn't read at night. Finally, they had gone to the doctor who had told them that, even though the child was clearly exhausted, there was nothing wrong with her. Her parents were at the end of their rope, her brother felt neglected, and Frances didn't sleep. The three of them went to see Mr. Miller together. After Mum and Dad had told him about what had been going on, he scolded them for not telling him sooner. That made Frances angry, because nobody should get to scold her parents. She shot him a look, but his smell didn't change, which made her feel frustrated. Mr. Miller sent the three of them straight to the school psychologist, Mrs. Fry.

Mrs. Fry was a young, gentle woman, who often brought her dog, a fluffy havanese called Sniggers, to work.

When Mrs. Fry called them inside, Frances went straight to Sniggers and laid down next to him. She snuggled close to him and deeply inhaled his smell.

Mrs. Fry laughed. "He's not exactly clean. He can't be smelling that good."

Frances shrugged. Burying her nose deeply into Sniggers' fur was a heavenly holiday for her. Sniggers just smelt of dog. His smell was entirely light and pure. It was amazing. She had spent a good part of last year trying to convince her parents to get her a dog, but she reckoned that she would need to bug them for at least another year before they eventually gave in. So maybe it wasn't so bad that she had gotten into trouble – at least it meant getting to spend some time with Sniggers. She'd have no trouble sleeping here, by him, she thought. She was almost desperate enough to ask Mrs. Fry if she could take a nap. Frances absent-mindedly registered her parents sitting down at Mrs. Fry's desk and starting to talk. She only looked up from Sniggers' fur when she heard her mum crying.

There was a soft, gentle, yet heavy odor coming from her mum. Frances carried Sniggers to the far corner of the room and pulled him onto her lap. She could still smell him that way, but she could also see and hear what was going on.

"I just don't know what I did wrong", Mum said with desperation, while accepting the handkerchief Mrs. Fry was handing her. "She used to be such a happy, curious child. And so good at school. Now she's miserable. And I don't know why. I feel like I've failed as a mother."

That was one of the more ridiculous things Frances had heard in her life. It was silly that her mum was blaming herself, even though it wasn't her fault at all. Why was she doing that? It was Frances's fault for being too sensitive. Frances's and, well...

"There's nothing you could have done better, dear", Dad told Mum, "We did everything. We took her to a doctor. We read her bedtime stories. We put on relaxing music. Our entire lives are basically revolving around helping that little girl sleep. Mrs. Fry, I don't know what else we could do. We're at the end of our rope."

Frances knew what her dad could do to make everything go away. To make the stench go away. To make it so that she could sleep again. Frances was only a child, but she was not stupid. She knew her dad kept doing something he shouldn't. Something that wasn't allowed. Why else would he do it in the middle of the night and come home wrecked with guilt? She'd been too scared to follow him, and too scared to snoop on him, because she didn't want her own smell to go bad. But she had her theories.

1. He was secretly a murderer. It makes sense because murderers murder at night, don't they? And they should feel guilty, shouldn't they?

2. He was secretly a spy and was feeling guilty because it was a secret and you shouldn't keep secrets from your family.

3. He was a descendent from a long line of wizards and had to do his magic at night so nobody found out.

"Frances?" Mrs. Fry could see her looking, taking an interest. Frances looked back for a second before burying her face in Sniggers' fur again. She liked Mrs. Fry. But she couldn't tell her any of this. Not in front of her parents. It would make her dad lie and the stench would get worse and then who would that help. Mrs. Fry cleared her throat and looked at Mum and Dad.

"Would it be all right if I talked to Frances alone for a minute?"

"Sure", said Dad, "would that be all right, Frances? We'd be just outside the door."

Frances looked up at him. "I hear the autumn air is good for your lungs", she said.

"What?", Dad frowned at her.

Mum put a hand on his shoulder. "It's all right, sweetheart", she told Frances, "we'll go for a nice autumn walk, won't we, Jeff?"

After they'd finally left, Mrs. Fry returned to her seat behind her desk. "Would you like something to drink? I even smuggled some orange juice in here."

"Can you open the window, please?", Frances asked instead.

Mrs. Fry frowned for a moment. "Of course,", she said.

Frances followed her to the window and looked outside. She took deep breaths and looked on, as her parents were leaving the grounds of her school. She could feel Mrs. Fry's hand on her shoulder. "Just don't lean out too far, all right?" Frances nodded.

"I'm okay now", she announced and walked back over to Sniggers, who was licking a bookshelf, "thank you for sending them away."

Mrs. Fry pulled her chair towards them. "Is it okay if I sit here?", she asked. Frances nodded. "Why weren't you okay when your family was here?"

Frances shrugged. "They smell really bad. I mean, at least my dad does. But my mum… Now she smells worse but she shouldn't. It's not her who's doing wrong."

"Then who is doing wrong?" Frances scratched Sniggers under his chin and looked down.

"I am. I'm all sensitive and wired wrong. That's what he said to my mum and she said I was wired different. But I don't want to be. But it's my fault, still."

"And what about your dad? Is he doing wrong?" Frances looked up at her. "I think so. But I don't know."

"What is he doing that you think might be wrong?"

She shrugged. "He just leaves at night. And I know he says he goes on walks, but I know he's lying." Mrs. Fry looked at her in wonder.

"How do you know he's lying?" Frances removed a tic from Sniggers' fur and frowned.

"Because when he comes back, I feel like I need to puke he smells so bad."

"And what does he smell of?"

"Rotten eggs, rotten milk, rotten meat."

Mrs. Fry takes a breath. "And is that why you can't sleep?"

"Yeah."

There's a lot of crying happening on their way home. Most of it done by Mum and Dad. Since their private talk with Mrs. Fry, the smell has started to lift, slowly, a little. Frances smiles.

The Scent of a Killer

By Nilanjana Banerjee

Avery's account
7ᵗʰ January, 2018

I never write. Last time I composed something were catchphrases for a contest, two years back. My sister, to this day, claims that the judge had fainted not because her sugar level fell, but my atrocious rhymes.

But miracles do happen, so, here I am with an ancient notebook, recording something beyond the mundane. I'm providing a detailed account on the recent happenings in this small quaint town that made their way to several newspapers.

I'm Avery Turner, twenty-four. I run a bakery with my big sister, Annisa. It pays fairly fair to earn us our daily bread. Dear Annisa was kind enough to spare me a decent room in her house where my part-time job is tutoring her kids, Ellen of twelve and Harry of eleven. My simple life revolved around the bakery and home until that day when things started getting complicated, with my town being guarded by the police because a serial killer was on the loose. Now that I look back and connect the dots, everything falls into place.

It started late December when the Festive Mood invades the realm of the Monotony Monster, spreading Christmas fragrance in air. However, last Christmas would make a difference and December wouldn't only commemorate Christmas but those little lives snuffed out. Our bakery is usually packed around this time. Plum cakes, pies and Christmas pudding amongst others, attract customers like fresh nectar-filled flowers do to the bees and butterflies.

One such bustling day before Christmas, the ambience was too big for the little town; I was home with treats for the kids. They get more sweets in their parents' absence. Annisa and her husband, Sam, were on a tour, returning on the Eve. When the oldies were around, we used the code "Mayday for a heyday", for untimely snack times.

The evening newspaper reported a six-year-old child's tragic death. Two more such mishaps concerning victims within the same age group followed, all in a ten-day span. Kevin, the first victim's body was discovered in his backyard; Fanny among the bushes adjacent to the town's park and George, at his dining table, when his parents weren't home. These children, like my nephew and niece, went to the same middle school. The police noticed a pattern in the deaths– every child had been choked and they had gingerbread fragrance sprayed all over them, and to everyone's horror, gingerbread cookies stuffed in their mouths.

Such an alarming news had everyone panicking. Inspector Ella Decker mentioned that there must be a common motive behind the murders, committed very cleverly. Sorrow overshadowed the town; the trio tragedy being discussed in every corner. It was a wicked mockery, leaving gingerbread scent and cookies, like an open challenge. It was discovered that the cookies were from our store. Inspector came down one day for "chitchat". Ellen and Harry were also asked if they had seen anything "weird" recently. It broke me to see them shaking in their shoes, terrified by the situation.

How could someone be so cruel? The kids shared a room and I took the couch there. I was too scared to leave them all night on their own. Every kid was glued to their guardian, none being left alone, unguarded for a moment. But the threat is unfathomable until danger knocks at your door. This fate befell me. Joe, a teacher from the school visited us on the 22nd afternoon, regarding the kids. They hadn't attended lessons for two days and it was the last day before winter break.

"Can I speak to the children?"

"By all means!" I went upstairs to fetch my angels. When I returned with them, Joe was rummaging through the backpack and our emergence startled the teacher and the backpack fell on the floor. For a split second I caught the glimpse of a pack of gingerbread cookies. The scent was quite fresh. A cold sweat ran down my spine. It was our product and to mourn those hapless children, I had decided to stop selling it for the year. Joe hadn't been to the bakery in a while and wasn't social enough to receive gifts. My mind was racing, my hands were cold. What would I do? The kids were already there and I couldn't possibly guess a psychopath's moves when two potential targets were in the room. I tried to maintain my composure and think. My phone was on charge on the kitchen counter, next to which Joe was seated. I realized that my children's safety was most essential.

After some small talk I hastily announced, "Look, champs! Break time. Let's go outside." Needless to say, they were bewildered; it was time for their favorite show.

Their surprise was soon upstaged by my terror when, supporting me, a grinning Joe said, "Ah, lovely idea. Why don't you go play while the elders chat?"

Realization dawned upon me. This time, I was the target.

Emily's account
1ˢᵗ December

My darling, You didn't deserve to die like this, sweet pea. You were the world to me. What am I to do with this life without you? How I told you time and again not to hurry while eating. But I understand it wasn't your fault, honey. Your friends are the culprits. You wanted to play with those kids, and you rushed through your gingerbread cookies. Their scent that once used to lighten up my spirits, has become a reminder of your absence. My blood boils every time the fragrance is in the air. How badly I hate it. But don't you worry, dearest. You will be avenged. Those responsible for your departure will be punished by the hand writing this note. I promise, angel.

I still remember holding you in my palms, you were so small! How I held you with my life, as if I were holding my own life in my hands. Your dad left, and I was shattered. But your sweet little face kept me going. How am I going to survive without you, honey? I recall cooking and baking for you, flicking dough on your nose. Oh, how you giggled... it rings in my mind as I write to you. How your face lit up, how excited you were every time I baked cakes, muffins, and...gingerbread cookies. I was shattered a second time when you left me forever and spent months in a trance-like suspended animation.

Gradually I came back to myself and saw clearly what had to be done. My resolve solidified with time. Your friends and those bakery sisters will pay for what they've done. I'll make sure of that with the last drop of my blood, the last breath I draw. The party will begin during the festive season. The best of times will unwittingly usher in the worst of times.

All my love,
Mommy

9th December

Dearest Beverly,

Our first target is down. That bloke Kevin didn't see it coming. Poor lad thought Miss Anderson wanted to "play".

"Why fear her? She'd never kill me, would she?" Ah, who knew retribution tasted so sweet. The time was perfect, Bevvie. I've been observing our targets very closely. I knew when this one would be alone and I know when the others will. I was scared. I'm not a murderer! I'm doing what's right. To gather courage, I asked Kevin if he had any gingerbread cookies; I was hungry... (for revenge). The boy went inside and returned with the box, and the moment I smelled it... you were all I could think of. That fragrance was mesmerizing; reminiscent of you. And then, I did it. Before leaving, I sprayed the gingerbread perfume all over him and stuffed two cookies in his mouth. I brought home the box. That's what drives me, the scent. It was your favorite. I feel like I can smell you, as though you're so near me but I can't quite pinpoint where.

Exactly a year ago you had left me. Payback period begins today. The first one has been successfully completed. Just you wait, sweetheart. The next blow will be soon delivered.

Love,
Mommy

14th December

Darling Bevvie,

The second quest has been a success. Fanny was happy to see that her class teacher had come to see her in the park. How trust can deceive one... It's true that ever since you left, she had been all alone; she couldn't mingle. That's what I used against her. I knew she used to be at the park when it was almost empty. Thereafter, throwing the ball in the hedges and putting her to eternal sleep was cakewalk. You know, sweet pea, my hands were shaking again while walking up to her. She was a sweet girl. I had to remind myself what I was there for. So, I yanked out the gingerbread perfume and inhaled the scent, your scent. And, I did it.

Love,
Mommy

18th December

Sweetheart Beverly,

This one was difficult, but, Mommy is Superwoman! When his parents weren't home, George had a babysitter, which caused the problem. But universe wants me to deliver justice for my darling, that's why his babysitter couldn't make it there today. Lucky for her. George was alone. Perhaps his mum tried to come home early, but, too late. Our next target lives a block away from the police station. I have to be careful. One bird is out of town. It has to wait. For now, only one target to hit. Avery Turner.

Love,
Mommy (Emily Josephine Anderson)

Avery's account (continued)

The kids were confused, but they're smart. They realized something was wrong. But no wrong move was allowed. I tried to play along with Josephine and nodded to my angels.

"Mayday on a grey day, remember?" I wasn't sure if they caught the hint, but one had to trust the gut. They gave me a meaningful glance and went out. Joe and I were alone now, and I had to buy time.

"Well, Avery, let's get down to business, shall we?" I couldn't hold it together anymore.

"It was you."

"Ha! Takes a killer to know a killer."

"What d'you mean? What'd I do?"

"What'd you do, eh? Remember killing my little girl?" She was stepping closer. "But she choked on her food."

"ON YOUR BLOODY COOKIE!" I trembled. She was even closer now. I tried to explain to her as calmly as humanly possible, standing inches away from a woman who had murdered three children in cold blood. I grabbed a vase but I couldn't hit someone deliberately. After what felt like eternity but was actually five minutes or so, she reached for my throat. I had no choice but to swing the vase at her head.

"BANG!" it went, but she was stronger than I thought. She recovered swiftly and before I could reach the door, her nails dug into my neck, the area I'm always panicky about; the region where my lymph nodes had once swollen. It was probably due to the panic rather than the injury that I fainted while I felt warm liquid trickling down my neck. I woke up in the hospital; my neck was bandaged. It hurt jolly good. Ellen and Harry were at my side and I could see relief wash over their faces when I looked at them and gave a thumbs-up.

Inspector Decker entered after she was notified that I was conscious. She related how my brave angels had rushed to the police station the very instant they stepped out of the house. The police reached on time when Josephine was in the process of finishing me. She was arrested. Perhaps she would be transferred to an asylum. I looked at my children, my eyes welling up. Those clever little ones had saved their aunt. I could barely move my head but I reached out for them and they clutched my hands. I gripped them back. Perhaps, for a fleeting moment I could relate with poor Emily Josephine Anderson.

L'ame du Parfum

By Vignesh Sivasankar

I promulgated the news and I've got bees surveilling my honeycomb. The quicker I trade, the sooner I can unload the burden off my shoulders. This isn't as easy as falling off a log. I got machinery, processors, computer systems, a database of suppliers and distributors, employees, a warehouse, and a front office. I need to box-up, gift-wrap, tie a ribbon, and get rid of an establishment.

In these thirty years, the company didn't procure reputation instead earned it. Tradesmen in the bazaar, folks in the perfume industry, and cologne lovers are acquainted with the brand. Loyal customers spritz our scent, froth our soaps, and daub our creams. The new owner has the advantage of this fidelity. When I was ten, I asked my father 'Why did you name it L'ame du parfum?'

'It's a French word. Which means 'the soul of fragrance.' Perfume companies name their products, either French or Italian. That's because the modern concept of perfume is from France and Italy, although some studies have shown ancient Mesopotamia used colognes! We can't name the brand in Sumerian, Babylonian, and Assyrian languages, right?'

His answers are always abundant. He's an uneducated knowledge bank. I chose the most flawed memory of my father and cling to it. I chose it now because, at that moment, he was the person he shouldn't have been.

'Whack me with your slippers, if ever again I ask you for a pocket money,' I said as I threw the leftover cash on his office desk.

On a gloomy weekday evening, when the machines rigged and ragged and employees worked their asses off to finish their respective tasks, I blasted. He was going through a few invoices. A few coins and crumpled old notes of fifty, twenty, and tens fell over his file. I've already spent the hundreds and five-hundreds.

'You don't have to vent your anger. You're my only son. I want you to be safe. I refrained you from going to that retreat is because I was scared something might happen to you. If it was a hill station here and there, I wouldn't have bothered. But your writer's club course was in the foothills of the Himalayas. Too far, too high! You might get inspired to write, but for a widower whose only son wants to take such a daring trip with a tent bag heavier than himself, it's challenging for me.'

'That doesn't mean you have to follow me right up to the snow-capped mountains to check on me if I'm fine or not! The same thing happened on my 10th standard school tour. You followed me to Coorg just to make sure I'm fine. I mean, who the hell stalks his son on his school excursion?!'

'Just to be sure if you're fine,' he said.

'I'm fine, daddy. I'm fine by myself. It's you who's creating a ruckus in my life by over-protecting me for anything and everything. You forced me to take up business administration after schooling even though you knew

I desired to become a writer. You spent money half-heartedly for my graduation in English literature. Your tantrums regarding your friend's son doing an MBA and looking after their family business or your colleague's daughter who has taken up engineering and settling in a high-flying corporate job were never-ending. Why can't I be different? I don't want to waste my life only to earn money. I wish to write. Although I might earn less, I'll be happy. Why can't you understand?'

'As a father, I always wanted the best for you. I'm an illiterate because my father wasn't financially sound. I stopped schooling when I was fourteen. I started working in menial jobs to earn money. Education was a far-fetched dream for me. When I'm well off now, I want my son to get the best of enlightenment and lead a better life by handling this stable business in the busy streets of North Madras than becoming an unshaven, liquor-smelling, sling bagged, beggarly novelist.'

'Are you challenging my ability to become a successful writer?'

'I didn't mean that. All I wanted was to'

'That's enough, daddy. That is all I wanted to hear.' Those were the last words that left my tongue. I stormed out of his office. Not just office, it is a combination of office, warehouse, manufacturing unit all put together in a dingy busy corner of Mint street, the longest street in India. I went home, packed my stuff in a suitcase with my passport, mobile phone, and left the city. I took some credit from my friends and reached Bangalore to start a new life.

With a BA degree in English literature, a raging desire to become a successful author, zilch money in my pockets, I roamed around the garden city for a job for the next six months. I got a job as a copy-editor in one of the English dailies. In the morning, I slogged myself to edit the articles and get them approved by other editors, and burning the midnight oil in finishing my novel.

In eighteen months, I got another job in Mumbai from a leading English daily to lead a team of copywriters. My manuscript was ready and with a few contacts which I have developed in the media industry, I submitted my proposal to many publishers. Rejection slips that I received could be bind into a hardcover manual. Some publishers were asking me for money to publish my work. How funny the publishing business has changed? Slogging for a couple of years in Mumbai, I wrote two other novels as well. One publisher accepted my third manuscript for a peanut royalty and I agreed. Within the next 2 years, four books that had my name as an author was published. The royalty I earned was much more than what my day job in Delhi offered me. I spent another two years in the literature heaven of India - Kolkata.

Daddy used to call me every day twice. Once in the morning before I start my work and once before I went to bed. For ten years I didn't go back to Chennai, haven't met my father even once. Yet, he called me twice every single day for 3652 days. I've never intended to call him even once. I want to prove my dreams are worth every pain. Last week he called on Monday, for the next two days there was none. On Thursday I got a call from his number but the person who spoke was Arumuga Chettiyar, my father's business manager who was working with us for the past 30 years.

'Appa is no more. He had a sudden cardiac arrest. We took him to the hospital, but they declared us brought dead. Could you please come down?' I left my errands in

West Bengal and dashed to Chennai. I completed the formalities and rituals as we cremated the body. I ought to sell his business and our property - the lonely independent house in the bustling market area. I have called an auction wherein the best entrepreneurs in the market are bidding to secure the perfume business. As I was about to interview the people from my father's office, Arumuga Chettiyar came with a notebook.

'Your father used to write this journal when an air of melancholy surrounded him. He did miss you a lot in these years. If you have time, read it,' he said. I flipped through the pages as his beautiful handwriting mesmerized me like the lustre of a pearl found in oysters. One page, one paragraph made me topsy-turvy.

"My wife passed away sooner than I expected. She wasn't able to bear the pain of childbirth. She gifted me a bundle of joy but she didn't join me to cherish the happiness. My little boy was like a cloud from heaven. He was soft and tender like a cotton dandelion. Unlike other babies, he wasn't smelling good. Naturally, he stunk. It wasn't his stool, his urine, or his vomit. My baby had a pungent rotten smell even after a bath. The doctors termed the condition as Trimethylaminuria, a rare genetic baby odor disorder. We're coastal people and love to eat fish, but that doesn't mean my child should have a fishy smell all through his life! We tried various treatments; all our efforts were mere vain attempts. My prince shouldn't grow up with psychological and social distress. So, an Ayurveda expert gave a few suggestions. One of them was to have a good diet. She proposed a diet rich in Vitamin B12 and probiotics. Allopathy doctors suggested expensive antibiotic tablets. To make him fragrant, I cut down all costs. I ate once a day. I went to bed empty stomach. I made sure his treatment is followed rigorously. Being single isn't difficult. Being a single parent with an infant is an endless battle. One day, an amazing piece of advice changed my life – have you tried 'activated charcoal' soap? During those days it wasn't available in the market as a finished good. So, I brought raw ingredients like soap base, charcoal powder, and peppermint essential oils to make one. It removed oil stains from my baby in a jiffy. The diet and supplements made sure hormones are altered and my little boy was smelling good in no time. He smelt pleasant. I sold the retained soaps for a good sum. That's where my business idea gleamed like a 100 watts' bulb. I procured natural herbs and essential oils at a cheap rate with my chit fund savings. I purchased a soap wrapping machine with the help of credit from my friends. It wasn't a risky affair. I don't have anything to lose. If that fragrance can save my child, it can help be build a business too, I thought. Thus, I started the brand 'L'ame du Parfum'. The soul of fragrance – my son. He is the soul of fragrance. He's the spirit and driving force upon which this business was created and is successfully running for so many years. The reason I'm successful in manufacturing and selling fragrances is not that people would like to smell good nowadays, or it makes them happy, or it's a perfect aphrodisiac. No, you idiots! Fragrance what I create is the love for my son. His soul is in everything I've created. I'm not a professional perfumer, I'm a seasonal perfumer who wanted the best for his son!"

A teardrop rolled down my cheeks and fell on the paper. The salty water smudged the ink where he wrote 'He is the soul of fragrance.' My self-assured hubris of best writer cascaded like a deck of cards. Look at his words puncturing your heart and shredding it into a million little pieces. I've been a reckless fool all these years. I was searching for a soul in my art by traveling to different locations, but I've failed to see that all along it was with me. The old man created a fragrance for me to dwell upon. I cancelled the interviews. I called-off the idea to sell my father's business and our house.

I shifted from Kolkata to Chennai in no time. I swirled my moustache like my father. I walked on those busy streets resembling him, where the onlookers gaped me with awe. I sat on my father's desk in his office. I uploaded all manual receipts and invoices on my new laptop in the digital version. It took me six months to revive the leftover business with a few technological advancements. But I did manage well. I still do write to express my thoughts. But my soul gets refreshed only when I smell the fragrance my father has left behind in this business. The innocent smile of my daddy flashes before my eyes, as the fragrance kindles my nostrils.

Reincarnation

By Rupsa Das

"Goodness," I swore as I looked at my watch. It was already past eleven, and I still had two more sheets to run through. After fifteen minutes, I was running down the empty staircase of the building, my footsteps echoing against the stark contrast of the winter night. I was met with a hopelessly deserted street as soon as I emerged, devoid of any kind of vehicles for me to hail. Running out of options, I booked a cab from my phone, and waited for it to arrive. A ding notified me that it'd be another ten minutes for the driver to reach. I walked up to a lamp post, with my hands inside my coat pockets, and tried to keep myself warm.

I was distinctly aware of the tingling sensation coursing through my body as I waited in the dark. It wasn't new; in fact, I would have been surprised if I wasn't on edge before meeting a complete stranger and riding with him. I scanned my surroundings, and felt myself sighing in relief when I couldn't find anyone.

However, my ears picked up something soon after. Footsteps, coming from my right. I looked over and could make out a tall, dark figure coming towards me.

I tensed instantly, holding my breath for no apparent reason. It was just a passer-by, another late-night office worker, I told myself. As the figure approached, my mind began conjuring up all sorts of incoherent thoughts. The figure – I realized it was man – walked just up to me, and stood there motionless. I looked straight ahead, but my attention was fixated on the stranger.

Was he going to attack? Was I in danger? A white flash in my peripheral vision told me he was using his phone. Was he calling his accomplice? The man hadn't shown any sign of violence, or even a threat, but the engulfing darkness around me wasn't helping at all. Maybe his calm demeanor was just a ruse; maybe he wanted me to relax before he pounced on me. And then it hit me. The obnoxious, sickly sweet fragrance.

All the alarms burst in my head as I tried to make sense of it. I realized I couldn't breathe – the air suddenly felt hot. I was visibly panting, as I felt his gaze on me. The smell penetrated into the deepest parts of my mind as my stomach tightened into knots. I was going to have a panic attack.

"Miss, are you okay?" a distant voice called out to me.

'It's not him', I screamed repeatedly in my head, 'it COULDN'T be him!'. I trembled, as I frantically tried to check my phone. I almost jumped out of my skin when the app notified that my cab was here. I looked around, and found a Corolla turning the bend of the road I was in. The tendrils of the man's fragrance were choking me, and I couldn't breathe. The cab stopped in front of me, and I hopped in without a second thought.

"Go!" I croaked to the driver. "Start driving!"

The driver gave me a weird look in the mirror, but I felt the car moving instantly. I looked outside the window to see the man looking back at me, with a questioning look. It wasn't him, after all. But the smell, god the smell. It was so alarmingly familiar. I felt nauseous as I leaned back against the seat and held my breath. I scratched my skin irritably, where I imaged the perfume was still lingering. I rested my head on my palms, and slowly let myself cry. I felt the hot tears streaming down my face, as the knots tightened further. I thought I was fine. I thought I was over this. But all it took was a sniff to tear apart a wound from eight years ago.

I watched from my window as my mom drove away. She had to attend an urgent meeting, so she left in a hurry. But my mom had called over my Uncle Theo to look after me while she was gone. I was only twelve, after all. I couldn't be just left behind alone. My eyes were still red and puffy, as I made sure again the room was locked. I had begged my mom to take me with her, but she had refused.

I heard Uncle Theo walking around downstairs, and I shivered. I never liked the man, and his huge belly and stinking breath only played a little part in this. He was in his mid-forties, same as my mom, but he never married. Something about 'doing whatever he wanted', and all that adult stuff. I remember when he used to buy me beautiful clothes when I was even younger. I absolutely loved those frilly frocks and denims. Till one day, when my mom was away and he was babysitting me, he came into my room and presented me with a new dress. I wasn't sure if it was a dress though, because the fabric was extremely scanty. It was lacey and black, and only covered the bare minimum of my body. He asked me to wear that and show it to him. I was reluctant at first, but he promised me ice cream afterwards, so I obliged. I walked in front of him as he scanned me all over. My chest wasn't that big, but it still held the fabric taut over that area. I was uncomfortable with my exposed thighs, but I really loved ice cream. Later on, when the show was over, he whispered in my ears to not to tell anyone about this. I figured the dress was costly and my mom would be angry on him, so I nodded. I heard a knock on my door and jumped.

"Chelsea? I know you're in there, baby, come out!" I heard Uncle Theo's raspy voice calling me outside. I shut my eyes tightly and prayed for him to go away.

"Chelsea, open the door." I was not going to let him in, ever again. Two weeks ago, he hurt me. He hurt me so badly that just thinking about it made me writhe in agony. The pain had subsided in my abdomen, but he had promised to come back. The images he took of my body were burnt in my head, when he threatened to show them to the world if I ever opened my mouth.

"Go away!" I screamed. "I don't want to see you! You hurt me!" I heard a rough chuckle from outside the door.

"Okay, okay, I'll be in the guest room if you need me, alright?" I heard his footsteps fading away as I relaxed. I was not, under any circumstances, going to go out of my room. I pulled out my drawing copy and scribbled all over the pages, trying to calm my nerves. I was constantly distracted by the fading bluish bruise on my inner thigh. His palms really were big. I went on scribbling and tearing the pages till I ran out of them. It was around eleven in the morning, but the skies were a dull grey. I hoped it didn't rain; mom would've taken longer to come home then. A little later, I was pacing in my room, trying to decide. I needed to go to the washroom desperately, but the problem was it was just beside the guest room, where Uncle Theo said he would be.

'That stupid man knew I had to come out for this,' I thought to myself. The constant anxiety wasn't helping either; I was almost trembling. I took a deep breath and opened the door an inch. He wasn't anywhere to be seen. I slowly walked out, looking at the long hallway in front of me. The washroom was at the end, and the guest room was to the left. As soon as I started walking down the hallway, the smell hit me. I used to love the fragrance; Uncle Theo had been wearing that for as long as I could remember. It was this sweet fruity smell, not too strong, but just enough to make you look at him. I could've recognized that smell anywhere, it smelled of love and home. Lately, however, it made my stomach churn.

A wave of nausea coursed through me as I inhaled the perfume. I had just put my hand on the doorknob, when I felt him behind me, standing too close. But how did he know I was there? I had walked as stealthily as possible! 'He was waiting for me!' I thought, as I turned to face him.

"Get away from me!" I screamed, as I went inside the washroom and tried to close the door. But he was thrice my size, and my efforts proved futile as he walked inside with me. The space drowned in that sweet, fruity smell, making me sick. I watched in horror as he smiled at me and closed the door behind him, locking it.

"Why are you so scared? I just want to love you!" he laughed, and walked closer to me. I backed up towards the wall, trying to stay out of reach. I felt like a helpless stag. I looked around, trying to find something, anything, to defend myself with. I backed into a row of shelves, as Uncle Theo continued walking towards me. Every inch of my body was telling me to run, but I was hopelessly cornered.

"There's no need to be scared," he said. He was so close I could smell the stink of his breath. "You're safe with me."

"You're going to hurt me again," I said through gritted teeth, not daring to meet his eyes.

"Have I ever?" he said, "No Chelsea, you're the love of my life." His words made my skin crawl.

I gasped when I felt his hand on my shoulder, gripping me tightly. "You're not going anywhere." I could feel the menace in his voice. I kept looking down at the floor, as I moved my hand behind my back, trying to reach the shelf. I felt my hand grasp a bottle, and held onto it tightly. "Come on, Chelsea, you know better than to resist. I still have the photos," he said, and inched closer.

I held my breath. I waited for a few moments, and jerked my knee up with all the force I could master, hitting him square between the legs. If I had taken a second longer, he would've grasped me and I never could've broken free. He slid down to the down, groaning loudly, as I uncapped the bottle of hair spray and pointed at his eyes. I almost dropped the bottle, as I sprayed all over his face, and bolted to the door. I could hear his screams coming from the bathroom as I ran to the entrance. I emerged outside, turning back from time to time to see if he was following.

To my utter disbelief, there he was, standing just at the threshold, glaring at me with bloodshot eyes. I just needed to run. All my senses blended as I lost track of where I was going. I crossed the street, screaming, when I heard a deafening screech. I stopped and looked back. A horde of people were standing with their backs facing me, and a truck was parked right behind them. My uncle was nowhere to be seen.

I slowly walked back to my house, and tried to see what the commotion was about. My face was streaked with tears, and I had trouble focusing, but I could make out the red on the street. It was a lot of red. I heard someone say something about a man limping across the street when the truck hit him. My brain was refusing to process anything that was happening. Even after that unfortunate turn of events, couldn't feel an inkling of sadness. I could see an ambulance and people running about, but it was all white noise.

Someone was trying to talk to me, asking me my name and where my mother was. I felt cold and numb, and the only thing I was aware of was the metallic smell of blood infiltrating my senses. And maybe it was just me, but I caught a whiff of something fruity along with it.

One would think that all the therapy, interrogations and even a funeral would make me believe that my uncle was, in fact, dead. But on nights like these, I still see him. When I'm alone and cold in the dark and a stranger walks by, wearing that same perfume, I feel my long-gone bruises throb. After I reached home at midnight, I was considerably calm. But I realized one thing he was right about. He was never going to let me go.

Inheritance

By Rohan Swamy

My earliest memory of Ammachi* was her sitting in the verandah on her rocking chair daydreaming. I would sit playing in the verandah with my Raggedy Ann doll that Appa* had bought during his trip to America. She would sit in her rocking chair, eyes closed, smile on lips, breathing gently and swaying to the songs of the wind. Ammachi, Appa, Amma*, and I stayed in a big house in Darjeeling then. I have fond memories of the house. My cousins, who stayed four houses down, would come every weekend and pester Ammachi to tell them stories of the goblin living in the Himalayas. She always obliged; even though it cut into her time of being with herself.

I didn't like to heckle her. We had our own unwritten rules, codes, and laws, which we made up. I would sit with my doll and play, and she would close her eyes and sit on the rocking chair and smile. It is here that we connected instantly. I inherited her idea of change. The modern world describes change as a movement from one state of being to another. Something that, in most cases, is irreversible. However, it wasn't the case with Ammachi. For her it was elastic. Everything could revert back to its original state after she had finished with it.

One time, when I was seven, Ammachi and I, ran into Amma's friend Radha on our way to the market. She did not like Ammachi but pretended to, on her face, as all grownups did. I do not remember the conversation they had in its entirety. There were references made to Ammachi's habit of sitting in the verandah and staring blankly into space, followed by snickers. What I do remember very well was Ammachi observing her silently when she laughed.

In the afternoon that day, I asked her about her habit and why Amma's friend laughed at her. Whenever I posed a question to Ammachi about life, her smiling face would, for a short instant, morph into a pensive one like the Sphinx before returning back to its original state. That day was no different.

She said, "Mina, you are very young but let me tell you something nevertheless. A day will come, many moons from now, when you shall find a world away from this world that we live in. It will be beautiful, as it will be magical. You will know the answer about my habit then."

I didn't understand what she said, but I was amazed to know that I would have my own world. Appa just had his own house and car but I would have my own world, complete with fairies and everything. I would have all the dolls too and the Raggedy Ann doll would be the head of all the dolls. We would all sit on the verandah and drink tea. What a glorious world it would be! As the years went by, the real world slowly weaned me away from Raggedy Ann, and the glorious tea parties that we were going to have. However, time and again I found myself escaping from the real world where changes were permanent, to the verandah searching for my own world that I was promised. The more I searched, the more I saw myself enjoying my own company. Along with that I found my drug – first in wax crayons and later on in the paintbrush.

On one of my painting sojourns in the verandah, Ammachi asked me the same question that Amma had asked many years back – 'Why do you not go and mingle with my cousins and partake in their conversations?'

I couldn't confess to her that I was searching for my own world, which I was promised as a child. I couldn't confess either that the mundane conversations about boys and their ways, and dresses and sequined jewelry didn't interest me. I couldn't confess that I felt out of place in my own place. Instead, I just looked at her and smiled. I suspect Ammachi understood all this. She took my hand in hers. They were wrinkled.

She proceeded to smoothen imaginary wrinkles on mine and said, "Mina, being alone doesn't make a person lonely. Remember that. Sometimes the worlds that we are born in are not the worlds that we seek. They are not our worlds. The worlds that we seek reside deep within us. We must journey deep within ourselves to find our worlds. Every day you spend alone in solitude you find a new marker that takes you closer to that world. Sometimes you even find a new friend. You also find a new truth and when you do, it brings immense joy. I know this is true for I have my own friends and they meet me in my own world. All I need to do is sit on my chair, close my eyes and smile and there I am, amongst my people – happy and carefree. I do not hanker for the snows of the past. Nor do I care for the old rains. As I said, when you reach your own world, every day you will find something new. I hope you will find it all with time."

Ammachi was right. All it needed was time. Art took

me to my own world. Even though I couldn't travel there the way Ammachi did, in the blink of an eye, I did manage to go there whenever I was painting. But all this came with costs. First school, and then college took me from the hills to the plateau and then the plains.

Distances froze Ammachi and me, but our worlds kept us connected. Often, I would catch a fleeting glimpse of her laughing and chatting with her friends. She would wave out to me when I sat in my little room in the college dorm, painting. We have our own codes and rituals. We have our own secrets too. - The world beyond this world; changes that are always elastic. – I'd hear her say to her friends as they drank tea and smelled the flowers in their gardens. The years that bought youth to me and color to my cheeks took the same away from Ammachi. It felt as though we were balancing the changing face of nature by shape shifting our appearances. Everything remained constant.

Then one day, five years back when I was 20, she passed away. She lived to be very old. Amma found her sitting with her eyes closed and a smile on her lips in her rocking chair on the verandah. After the usual hullaballoo associated with deaths, peace prevailed. Just like her life, her funeral too took place quietly. It was in sync with her ways and the ways of her world. This year when I went home during the monsoon holidays, I found Amma in deep conversation with Juggi – the rag and bone man. She wanted to dispose of Ammachi's old chair. I wondered what Ammachi would think of it. A part of me wanted to protect her legacy but I remembered her words – I do not hanker for the snows of the past. A deal was struck and I saw Juggi take the chair away to the slaughterhouse. Far away Ammachi sat with her friends, drinking buttered tea and laughing – least affected by the loss of her rocking chair.

Later that evening as I sat in the verandah with my paintbrush and paper lost with my people in my world, I saw Ammachi with her friends laughing and drinking buttered tea. It was just as I had imagined. Moments later the skies crackled and the first rains came. Ammachi waved out to me from her world. I waved back. I looked at her and smiled.

She smiled back. "Don't care for the old rains," she shouted. Her friends laughed. I laughed too. Then they all went away back to their own world, laughing and singing. And amidst the first rains of the monsoons, I smiled, closed my eyes and returned to mine.

Glossary:
*Ammachi – Grandmother
*Appa – Father
*Amma – Mother
*Verandah – porch

Home is where the heart is

By Gowri Bhargav

"**P**ushpa, add some more ghee to the venpongal. And don't forget to add some extra cashews," said Ramanujam to his wife. Every Sunday Ramanujam's friends gathered in his house for breakfast when they had a gala time catching up on interesting news that they wanted to share as they had breakfast and coffee.

Ramanujam was a retired headmaster. His wife Pushpa was a music teacher and a wonderful cook. They had been married for over thirty years and lived in Triplicane, Chennai which is home to the renowned Parthasarathy temple and other places of worship for the Hindus. It is a heritage town with many century old row houses and narrow streets. Being dominated by the Hindu Brahmin community it is a hub for all cultural activities like music, dance and religious activities. The Ramanujams had a son who worked for a reputed software company in New York. He was married and settled there. The Ramanujams had never had an opportunity to go to the US. Ramanujam always dreamt of going and settling there. His son had recently purchased a huge five-bedroom villa in New York which had made Ramanujam's dreams even rosier.

"Pushpa, once we go to New York, you can continue teaching music to desi children there. You can also make those tasty Sambhar and Rasam podis and sell it in grocery shops. I'm sure it would become a great hit. And as far as I am concerned, I can tutor math and science to high school students," he would always tell his wife.

"Why should we go and settle in a foreign soil? This is our home. This is where we got married and raised our family. I don't think it will work out", she would remark.

"Come on Pushpa. This is such a dirty place. Every day I have to scream at the garbage truck guy for parking his truck here. Ew, that nasty smell! And those vegetable vendors - they come screaming across the road asking people to buy vegetables. The kulfi wala – during the night when I am about to catch some sleep, he starts ringing the bell like a fire engine. I just want to get away from all this. Moreover, our son has built such a huge mansion so that we could also live with them. It's time we went there."

"Hmm! Whatever you say. Anyway, I will follow you wherever you go."

Pushpa's entire life revolved around her husband. A very devoted wife she would wake up early in the morning, finish her puja, cook breakfast and lunch and go to the temple to volunteer. In the afternoon after having lunch, they would spend an hour or two chit-chatting. In the evening her students would start trickling in slowly to attend music classes. Around 8 PM, once all the classes got over, they would have dinner together and go to bed. This was their usual routine. They both loved each other. But they were not like the couples shown in movies. He had never told her how much he loved her and nor had she. They just loved each other, that's it! It was an unassuming pure love.

It was the month of December which meant the Tamil calendar month of Margazhi for the people in Tamilnadu. And Triplicane especially wears a festive look during this time. Colorful rangolis are drawn in front of houses and groups of people can be seen singing songs and bhajans as early as 5 a.m. in the morning. Pushpa too was an active member in such groups. And as for Ramanujam he didn't like being woken up early in the morning.

"Oh God! I understand these people are greatly devoted to you. But does that mean they have to sing throughout the day in full volume? I am unable to get some peaceful moments for myself. I am just waiting for my son to invite us to the US. As soon as the green card application gets approved, I want to fly away to my land of dreams with my wife and lead a peaceful quiet life there."

One morning in December, Ramanujam was sipping his coffee and reading the newspaper when the phone rang. It was his son who had called to inform that the green card had been approved for Ramanujam and Pushpa. They could fly to the US now and live there for as long as they wished. This was the day Ramanujam had been waiting for. He wanted to go - away from this humdrum. He along with Pushpa could travel to all those exciting places with his son's family, tutor students and also have fun narrating stories to their granddaughter.

"Pushpa, Pushpa! Didn't I tell you? Finally, our dreams are going to become a reality. Let's start our shopping right away. We have many things to buy. First we need to buy large suitcases for ourselves." Pushpa didn't seem very excited. However, she could adapt to any place and any situation as long as her husband was with her. So deep was her love and she was extremely contended with whatever she had. She was just sixteen when she had married him. Her parents had expired at a very young age. Ever since, her whole life revolved around her husband. He was her friend, philosopher and guide. Ramanujam also had never spent even a single day without Pushpa. She was his world. They were not like the couples of today who like to showcase their love for each other.

It was one Vaikunta Ekadashi day in December. The Ramanujams followed the practice of observing fast on the day of Vaikunta Ekadashi every year. Vaikunta Ekadashi – An auspicious day when many people observe fast the entire day for Lord Vishnu. Pushpa spent the entire day singing songs and chanting hymns to the Lord. Ramanujam also chanted a few hymns. But he could not concentrate as he constantly thought about the foreign trip. In the night after having a telephonic conversation with his son regarding the documents required, they went to sleep. They had to wake up early the next day.

The next day was Dwadashi. After offering prayers to God an elaborate meal is served. A hungry Ramanujam woke up at 4 AM. Usually Pushpa always woke up earlier than him. And on such days when they observed fast Pushpa usually prepared a sumptuous meal early in the morning. But on that day, she seemed to be sleepy. Ramanujam got ready and waited for his wife to wake up.

By then it was already 5 AM and she hadn't woken up. He went beside her and uttered her name. But she did not budge. And then when he shook her, she seemed to be speechless and still.

"Pushpa……, Pushpa…", he uttered her name several times in vain. The whole world seemed to crash before his eyes. He immediately called his family doctor who came and declared her dead. She had suffered a massive heart attack. Ramanujam was left in a complete state of shock.

"How could this happen? How can Pushpa leave me just like that? Is it true? No, No, this can't happen," he kept repeating the same lines over and over again. His neighbors tried to console him. The next day his son flew down to Chennai. By then all relatives too had gathered. Ramanujam was in a complete state of despair. All the rituals and the last rites were performed.

"Appa! The green card papers are ready. I plan to take you to US with me. It will help you overcome the grief. Moreover, you also wanted to come and settle in the US," said his son. Ramanujam would be left in a state of solitude if he chose not to go. He agreed and packed his bags. He kept a photograph of Pushpa dressed in all her wedding finery. He also took a silk saree and a few things of hers that he cherished. It was already three weeks since Pushpa had left him. Ramanujam settled all the bills and was all set to travel to the US. His whole life seemed to have been shrouded by a cloud of darkness.

"If only Pushpa had been around, we both would have travelled together," he kept telling himself as tears trickled down his eyes.

Long Island, New York

Krishna, Ramanujam's son was a software engineer. His wife worked as a nurse in a hospital nearby. Their only daughter Deepa studied in grade three in the county public school. Ramanujam loved spending time with his granddaughter. He enjoyed telling her stories. His son and daughter-in-law tried to make him as comfortable as possible. They even subscribed to the Tamil channels so that he could watch his Tamil shows when they were away at work. Ramanujam tried to keep himself occupied.

However, whatever he did, he was constantly reminded of his dear Pushpa. She had been his soul mate. He tried rewinding those wonderful moments with her. Death is inevitable but the harsh reality takes quite a long time to seep in. Or maybe it never does. His son tried to cheer him up by telling him that time is a great healer. Soon at the onset of spring he could join the senior citizens club and spend time there. But Ramanujam felt as though a part of his soul was already dead. Could anything be normal ever again without Pushpa?

The word Pushpa meant flower. She was like a flower that had bloomed every single day to fill his life with fragrance. Pushpa was the very reason he had enjoyed everything in his life. Without her his life had plummeted into an abyss. It had been almost a month since he had come to the US. He did not wish to stay there any longer. He longed to go back to his dear old Triplicane. He yearned for all those sights, smells and sounds. Every memory made in that house was infused with the fragrance of Pushpa. He wanted to spend the remaining years of his life cherishing all those nostalgic moments. And that would be impossible if he stayed here in the US. He had made up his mind and asked his son to book a flight back to Chennai.

"But Appa! How can you stay alone? Moreover, settling in US has always been your dream. Without Amma it will be difficult for you," Krishna seemed surprised by Ramanujam's decision. But Ramanujam was not ready to listen and his son did not wish to force him. He booked his ticket to India.

Soon Ramanujam arrived in Chennai. As he unlocked his house, he had a strange feeling that Pushpa was still around. He seemed to feel her presence. As he drank his coffee it reminded him of the sweet conversations they used to have in the mornings. The Parijath (Night Jasmine) tree in the backyard swayed with the breeze and he felt as though Pushpa was trying to embrace him. After all a house is not just a house. It is a home that breathes with all the events it witnesses. Now his breath seemed to be infused with memories of Pushpa. He now did not wish to go anywhere. This was his house and... Pushpa's.

A house infused with the fragrance of Pushpa which was incomparable to none other place. Ramanujam spent the remaining few years of his life reliving the nostalgic moments in solitude. Though Pushpa was not physically present, her thoughts entwined his mind and he could always sense her fragrant presence throughout the house.

Glossary:
*VenPongal: Venn (Tamil word for white) is a popular savory dish in south Indian homes. It is typically served

as breakfast served as a special breakfast especially in Tamil Nadu. It is usually served with sambar and coconut chutney.

*Sambar / Rasam - South Indian stew made with lentils, tamarind, herbs, spices, Podis – Powders

*Vaikunta Ekadashi - Vaikuntha Ekadashi is one of the important and auspicious days for Hindus. It is dedicated to Vishnu. It occurs in the Hindu calendar, in the month of Margashirsha (between December and January). When observed, it bestows liberation from the cycle of birth and death. Dwadashi – Dwadashi (Sanskrit for Twelve) is the twelfth lunar day (Tithi) of the shukla (bright) or krishna (dark) fortnight, or Paksha, of every lunar month in the Hindu calendar.

Mambally Bapu takes the cake

By Santhini Govindan

It was mid-morning on a sunny November day. Mambally Bapu bent low, was busy tossing coconut shells into his borma (cob oven) when his young nephew came running up to him.

"The carriage of the big saip* from Anjarakandy is coming this way," he announced breathlessly.

"What? Really?" Bapu straightened up with a quick jerk.

"Bring me a clean thorthu*," he snapped, as he dashed to the water tap to wash off the soot that caked his hands. "Hurry!" Bapu made sure that he was quite presentable by the time the saip's horse drawn carriage clip clopped into his premises. He was well aware that he really needed the patronage of the British saips to make a success of his fledgling business venture.

Three years earlier, in 1880, Mambally Bapu, a businessman, had returned to his hometown Tellicherry in the north of the Malabar district, from the British province of Burma where he was engaged in shipping milk, tea, and bread to British troops stationed in Egypt. While he was in Burma, Bapu had learnt how to bake bread, buns, and a variety of biscuits. These food items were in great demand among the white sahibs who ruled the British colonies. Bapu, who was tired of living in Burma, and quite homesick too, decided to go back home and establish a small bakery there. He was confident that he would find enough customers among the small contingent of British soldiers stationed in the Tellicherry Fort, and in the town of Cannanore, eleven miles away, which was the British military headquarters on India's west coast.

So, Mambally Bapu, along with his nephews, established 'The Royal Biscuit Factory' in Tellicherry.' Initially, Mambally's main product was bread, or 'kappal roti' (bread for ships) and his bread dough, made by crushing wheat in crude stone grinders, was fermented using local toddy. Since Tellicherry was a busy port, ships that routinely anchored there stocked up on Mambally's soft, spongy bread which kept well during long journeys.

Eventually, Bapu began to recreate some of the recipes he had discovered while he was in Burma, and soon his little bakery was producing forty different varieties of bread, rusks, and buns. The locals of Tellicherry, who had lived through a severe famine five years earlier, also queued up to buy staples from Bapu's bakery - bread, and 'lotta,' a small, light, round hard bun with a very long shelf life that even laborers could carry around easily. Bapu stood at a distance and watched respectfully as Murdoc Brown, who owned a large cinnamon plantation in nearby Anjarakandy got down from his carriage. As the tall Englishman approached, Bapu bowed politely.

Murdoc Brown knew a smattering of Malayalam, and Bapu had learnt how to converse in simple English during his stay in Burma, so the two men were usually able to communicate without much difficulty. But to Bapu's surprise, on this particular day, the English sahib was not, as usual, interested in uttering pleasantries or in sniffing and browsing through Bapu's baked goods. Instead, he took out a round tin from the basket he was carrying, and placed it on the small, rickety table in Bapu's shop. Bapu watched curiously as Murdoc Brown prised open the lid of the tin. Once the lid was open, a delectable, fruity aroma floated out from it. Bapu's nose, well-known for its uncanny ability to pick out myriad scents, began to twitch immediately.

"What do you have in that tin?" he asked Murdoc Brown curiously. Murdoc took a round, brown object, shaped like a large bun, out of the tin.

"It's something I brought back all the way from England for you to see," he said. "It is a Christmas cake."

"Kay-k?" Bapu rolled the unfamiliar word on his tongue. "I know that you are an excellent baker. I want you to try and bake a Christmas cake for me, just like this one!"

Mambally Bapu eyed the cake doubtfully. "But today is the first time that I have ever seen a kayk," he replied honestly. "I don't know anything about making one at all."

Murdoc Brown waved his hand airily. "Don't worry about that!" he said jauntily. "I'll give you clear instructions on how to make a Christmas cake. And with your knowledge of baking, you should have no trouble at all in baking one with a similar flavour. But first, I want you to taste a piece of the cake." He cut a slice from the rich plum cake and handed it to Bapu.

Bapu bit into the cake tentatively, and his eyes mirrored surprise and delight as the moist cake dissolved on his tongue, and its delightful flavour spread in his mouth. Then, Bapu listened carefully as Murdoc Brown held forth for the next ten minutes on the method of making a Christmas cake.

First, he listed the ingredients that went into making the cake – flour, butter, eggs and sugar. As Bapu noted down the measurements, the Englishman explained that the dry fruit in the cake would have to be soaked for at least two or three days in brandy or wine before it was added to the cake batter. Before Bapu could ask for a list of the dry fruits required for the cake, Murdoc gave him a packet containing sundry ingredients like cocoa, dates, raisins, aromatic sticks of cinnamon from his own estate, and other dry fruits.

"These items are an integral part of a Christmas cake," he said. "You can use them. As for the brandy, I suggest you use the excellent French brandy that is available in Mahe."

Bapu had several more questions on cake making for Murdoc, and the Englishman answered them patiently. Before he got into his carriage, Bapu had promised Murdoc that he would try out his recipe, and make the cake before Christmas. Soon after Murdoc Brown left his premises, Mambally Bapu set out for the town of Dharmadam, about five miles away from Tellicherry, to meet a blacksmith who lived there.

Bapu explained to the blacksmith that he needed a heavy, circular cast iron pan with a flat bottom to make a special delicacy in his borma for the rich English saip of Anjarakandy. The blacksmith agreed to make the cake mould, and then Bapu decided to go to the French colony Mahe to procure the French brandy recommended by Murdoc Brown. But as he was going along, Bapu suddenly had a brainwave. Instead of buying and using expensive French brandy in his cake, why shouldn't he use a full – bodied local country liquor that he had savored and enjoyed himself?

The brew he had in mind was one made from Kadali-pazham, a variety of locally grown banana, and cashew apples, or the fruits that cashew nuts are attached to. It had a warm, sweet taste that Bapu felt would perfectly complement the sun-dried fruits going into in the plum cake. The more Bapu thought about the Christmas cake he had been commissioned to bake, the more enthusiastic about it he became. He threw himself wholeheartedly into the task, and carefully collected the choicest cloves, cardamoms, nutmegs, ginger, almonds and raisins from nearby plantations. Then the actual task of making the cake began. But alas! Though Bapu followed Murdoc Brown's recipe (and verbal instructions) his initial attempts at baking a good plum cake were disastrous – the cake was either too hard, or uncooked in the center though brown and crisp outside.

Bapu was disappointed, but not discouraged. He realized that his cake was not rising properly because the heat in his arched, cave-like cob oven was not even, so he carefully rearranged the coconut shells in it. The fruits and nuts in his plum cake were sinking to the bottom of the cake because he had forgotten to follow one of Murdoc Brown's important instructions – all the dried fruit had to be coated in a few spoons of flour before being added to the cake batter. This helped them to stick to the batter while baking, and prevented them from settling at the bottom of the cake pan.

Over the next week, Mambally Bapu immersed himself in the art of making plum cake. He experimented, measured and powdered all the spices himself, and then sniffed the mixture carefully to make sure that all the subtle aromas were well blended. He stirred and whisked, and added just enough of his robust country liquor to the fragrant cake batter to make it rich and appetizing. As local people walked past Mambally Bapu's Royal Biscuit Factory, they got the whiff of an unfamiliar, but heavenly fragrance. Many people approached Bapu, standing quietly beside his borma.

"What kind of biscuits are you baking today, Bapu? They smell just delicious! Can you share some with us too?" Bapu shook his head and waved his hands firmly.

"I'm not baking biscuits today – I'm busy making a unique new delicacy that has been specially ordered from me by the saip from Anjarakandy."

When he was perfectly satisfied with the texture, flavour and fragrance of his boozy plum cake, Bapu gave his family members and all his nephews a piece of cake to taste. Everyone appreciated the cake which was soft, moist, and a perfect balance of sweetness and spiciness. Bapu was finally satisfied with his creation, and he sent one of his nephews to Anjarakandy to inform Murdoc Brown that he had made a plum cake for him. He would be pleased to present it to him on the 20th of December – five days before Christmas.

There was an air of excitement and expectancy at Bapu's Royal Biscuit Factory when Murdoc Brown arrived on the 20th. The Englishman smiled at Bapu and rubbed his hands together.

"Let's see what you have to show me," he said genially. As Bapu brought out the plum cake he had made, Murdoc Brown sniffed the air appreciatively.

"Your cake certainly smells wonderful," he remarked

cheerfully. Bapu cut a slice of the plum cake and offered it to the English sahib. "I didn't use the French brandy you recommended in my cake," he explained tentatively, "and I added some extra spices that I thought would add to its general taste and flavour."

Murdoc Brown bit into the slice of cake, and he closed his eyes as he tasted it. Mambally Bapu's body was stiff and tense as he watched the Englishman's expression anxiously. Would the English saip appreciate the delicate and piquant flavour of the unique bouquet of spices that he had combined with such thought and care?

Murdoc Brown opened his eyes, and licked his lips. "Give me another slice of your cake," he said to Bapu. Mambally Bapu smiled delightedly, and hurried to oblige.

"Your plum cake is one of the best cakes I have ever had," Murdoc Brown said to Mambally Bapu with a chuckle. "In fact, it is so good that I won't buy just one cake! I am going to order a dozen more!"

As Mambally Bapu hurried away to fulfill his first orders for the first cake he had baked in his little borma, he didn't realize that he was creating culinary history. He had baked India's very first Christmas cake! Not surprisingly, the fame of Bapu's delectable, fragrant plum cake spread. It soon became a hot favorite with the locals, and his business flourished. In later years, Bapu's descendants set up bakeries in different cities of their state, and today, more than 135 years after Bapu made India's first Christmas cake, there are up to 40 bakeries in every panchayat of Kerala. Tellicherry, (now Thalassery) leads India's cake industry, and international customers flock to order Christmas cakes from the town's bakeries. The fragrance of one little cake, baked as an experiment in a crude cob oven more than a century ago, has truly spread across the world...

Glossary:
*saip – colloquial pronunciation of 'sahib'
*thorthu – thin, white cotton towel

The Guest

By Isabelle Jeong

A friendly smile and a warm greeting. Hazel pushed up the corners of her mouth with her two fingers. It had been exactly two months since she started working at the front desk of Rosewood Hotel, her each and every day bored by the rigid structure of her work schedule. It was almost enough for her to quit - almost.

The paychecks kept her going. Besides, her life was already a constant, mechanically repetitive recurrence of routines anyway, with or without the job. The last time spontaneity was a part of her life was back in high school. With a particular person. And quitting now would only introduce unwanted disruption - she'd already gotten used to the artificially sweet scent of warm coconut and fresh lime that wafted through the first-floor lobby. When she heard a familiar creaking sound from the hotel entrance, she instinctively faced the glass door held open by a colleague, her eyes naturally falling onto the two guests who were stepping into the hotel.

As they walked closer towards the front desk, into the visible range of her eye-sight, she could feel her friendly smile deforming into a melted mixture of flustered confusion and burning humiliation, along with a slight hint of sentimental delight. It was her ex. She hadn't seen Jane in a while, but she could still recognize her silhouette from a distance. Just about everything was the exact same as she remembered her to be, almost as if she'd just walked out of that time. Her hair was still a long, dark brown that complemented her olive skin. She was still tall and slim, with curves in which her waist cinched into her already thin figure.

The one thing she didn't recognize about her was that she had someone else by her side. She quickly smoothened her shirt with her hands, dusting off any lint she could spot in her peripheral, as she continued eyeing the two that walked in. It was a high school fling – it wasn't meant to be serious. But perhaps it was the nostalgic appeal of the act of falling in love for the first time, that was so impressionable that it left seemingly permanent scars that never faded away, even after all that time. Her hands gently pressed the top of her stomach, slowly moving up and down as she breathed in and out.

And how long had it been? Years. She didn't know exactly how many years it's been, but it was nonetheless enough time for one to let go and move on from. So, she must've moved on. Her heartbeat was loudly ringing in her ears, creating a pulsing sensation that passed through every part, every nerve of her body. She straightened her posture and flashed a smile, assuring herself that she'd be fine, that she'd already moved on.

"Good afternoon. Welcome to Rosewood Hotel." Her words were followed by a familiar voice that she hadn't heard in years - low, but soft. She noticed a pungent, powdery odor that came from the woman that stood next to Jane. She remembered that Jane used to have a distinct, signature scent.

Disappointingly, it was now undetectable, over-powered by the scent of Jane's friend. "-room service? Just a small bouquet of roses and some wine, please." Jane's voice snapped her out of her thoughts.

"Of course," she smiled reflexively.

"Is there anything else I can do for you?"

"No, thank you." Jane smiled - but it wasn't the kind she was used to. It was polite, mature, distant. The in-differently curved lines of her lips drew a firm, familiar yet foreign line between herself and Jane - a line that told her they were no longer acquainted. A line that was once crossed, but was never to be crossed again.

"Great. I hope you enjoy your stay."

The collective sound of their voices mushed into the background as distant mumbling. They disappeared to the hallway behind her towards the elevators, their shoes uniformly made clicking sounds against the pol-ished floor. Fighting temptation, her eyes did not turn to follow those footsteps. Instead, she closed them, waiting for the opening sound of the elevators. Then, she heard an unfamiliar, sharply high-pitched voice that flung her eyes open.

"Do you know her?" It was Jane's girlfriend. She froze - nervous, unable to decide if she wanted to hear what would come next.

"Yeah," she heard Jane say. She almost started to smile as she thought of the possibility that maybe, maybe she was remembered - quite fondly - by her. Perhaps, she, too, had occasionally reminisced about what had happened between them, plausibly, with adoration, and possibly, with affection.

"We went to the same high school."

It was a long shift. Tonight, she felt like drinking, for no particular reason at all. She shared brief goodbyes with her colleagues and went to the nearest bar she could find. As she walked in, she could smell a puff of alcohol, followed by a mix of perfumes that people wore - an overarching, strong, powdery musk decorated with scents of rose, jasmine, and some other florals she recognized but couldn't quite put a finger on. She sat herself down at one of the stools and ordered a margarita. In a few minutes, the cloudy, lime-colored drink was brought out. She could smell the bitter scent of tequila, the salty scent from the rim of the glass, and the sharp scent of alcohol, as she brought it to her mouth to take a sip.

Something inside her had split open. Maybe it was the wound that never got a chance to heal - after all, she never really tried, as if to rebel against the notion that time would fix her problems. She'd left those as they were, as if to treasure them. They were indeed part of the memories she'd frequently look back on. It was embarrassing. That she was so nervous when she first saw her walking into the hotel, that she felt a familiar set of emotions bubbling inside of herself when she heard her voice again for the first time in so many years, that she was somehow excited to hear what their past meant to her. That she, after all this time, was not over her. She turned her head away from her half-empty drink. Since it no longer entertained her, she was hunting something else down to fixate on.

The bar was nice. It was kind of dark, dimly lit with mahogany-red lighting. There were light bulbs shaped like teardrops that dangled from the ceiling, hanging over her head. Fancy enough to stay attentive to momentarily, but not for too long. She then noticed a pair sitting right next to her, kissing rather passionately. When something about them seemed oddly familiar - perhaps it was the invasively strong scent of perfume that she'd recognized from somewhere - she squinted in an attempt to see clearer. It was the woman she saw in the lobby earlier. Jane's current girlfriend. With someone other than Jane. She brought her hand up to hide the gasp that escaped her mouth.

Hazel stood in front of the hotel room, rigidly, face-to-face with the door that, if opened, would lead to Jane's hotel room. Shaking profusely, she lifted her hand to the door. When she knocked, she could hear faint noises from across the door, getting louder as she stood in the corridor in silence, until the door finally swung open.

"I just wanted to say - I know it's none of my business, but, I thought, that maybe you needed to know-" she paused to catch her breath, then continued. This time, she looked at her straight in the eye. "Your girlfriend is cheating on you."

"My girlfriend?"

"Yes, I saw her at a bar with someone else, they were-"

"Wait, wait. You must have misunderstood. I'm not dating her. I haven't dated anyone since-" Jane abruptly stopped, as if it was a knee-jerk reaction. She smoothly continued, "Well, I'm not dating her."

"But the wine and flowers?"

"We're just hooking up."

"Oh, I didn't know that you two were..." she paused shortly, attempting to find the right word to follow herself up with. As she looked for the word in the dark abyss of her mind, she sensed the ever-growing distance between herself and the one who stood in front of her, staring into her eyes. Her thoughts were leaving her own body behind, slowly drifting into an unknown void. The deafening silence was ringing in her ears, her parted lips were frozen in time, and her gaze pierced through the tense air between herself and Jane. She then whispered, "non-exclusive" - the last sound from her lips filling the room with a sharp, hissing echo.

Those were the last words she'd said to Jane before she had pulled her close. There were so many unsaid words she had always swallowed in front of her - out of pride and fear – that were uncontrollably spilling out, without her even having to speak a single one. Every light, feathery touch was her guiltily admitting she'd always been attracted to her, every breath she took in between each touch was her confessing she'd been longing for this very moment, and every prolonged, breathless touch was her declaring she'd miss how they used to be.

Each time their lips were drawn together after being parted for a quick second, she knew that she had waited for this moment her entire life - it was as if she was being rewarded for all the sleepless nights she had spent on Jane, crying. She knew, that she'd shamelessly dreamt of this very moment of reuniting with her - an alluring vision, produced by the artistic grief of her own mind, that never seemed likely to come true. She didn't know how long it had been, how long she'd been getting used to the soft sensation of Jane's lips on hers - it was breathless, like a dream, no, it was much, much more than what she'd ever dare to dream of. It felt almost too good to be true. She pulled away from Jane's arms, tearing herself away from her grip. She fumbled towards the door after murmuring a short, barely audible "sorry" in her direction.

Right when she shut the door behind her, the clicking sound of the door being locked helped her finally comprehend what had just happened. The abrupt ending of Jane's touch was softly lingering on her lips, a remnant that was there to perhaps remind her that this would be the last time she'd see her in that way - in the way that somewhat resembled how they used to be. Somewhat, but not quite. Jane looked like her. She dressed like her. She even talked like her - but her scent was completely different.

The person she loved, the one she'd countlessly fallen in love with over so many years of being separated, smelled like a rich blend of vanilla flower, shampoo, freshly-cleaned laundry, and a slight hint of sweet bubblegum. It would spread everywhere Jane went, leaving an intoxicating trail that lured in anyone who had even just a whiff of it. The very symbol of her first love and her first heartbreak.

The embodiment of the aftermath of it all. Jane's scent was like this when they first met, shy, and withdrawn. Her scent was like this on their first date, when she became increasingly bold and affectionate. Her scent was like this on the day of their breakup, when Hazel had cried on her brutally welcoming shoulders. That was how she'd always been. Yet, the woman she'd just kissed smelled like nothing at all.

As nothing as nothing could get - the vacant bareness of a blank slate, the very absence of the concept of a scent. As if that magical scent had never even existed. It was then when Hazel realized, she would no longer yearn for Jane, but rather, mourn for the one she'd lost to the cruel depths of time.

Cotton Candy

By Fiona Ballard

T he view from the window stretched out far across the Arabian Sea proudly displaying its Dhow sailing ships that had zig zagged their trading routes for centuries. Muscat was at its hottest, with temperatures soaring. Regrettably the safe secure world of two little brothers was about to end catapulting them into a vortex of life changes overnight. With the disappearance of their parents, Rashid, barely six years old and Malik four, had been far too small to fully comprehend the adult complications involved.

Malik had clung to a hazy childlike recollection about that fateful day, years later he found it buried deep down in his subconscious. He recalled being ushered into an overly hot room at home by Aunt Onecia and Uncle Tariq. Strangely on the day in question, there had been no air conditioning running, as that had always been his special job to turn it on. Every morning his Father would ask him to go and press the big green "on" button. If Mum and Dad had been at home that day, the air con would have been on its highest setting from dawn. But oddly it was turned off.

Seated side by side on the large rust-colored cushions

of the bamboo sofa, holding hands primarily for comfort, they could not remember being naughty that morning, were they in trouble? Why was Aunt Onecia anxiously pacing the floor, adding to the tension in the room,
making them more nervous? They cast a knowing look
at each other again confused and just couldn't work it
out. Awaiting Uncle Tariq to finish using the bathroom,
he walked into the room tucking himself into his brown
baggy trousers in a childlike manner. Typically, the boys
stifled their sniggers looking from one to another be-
mused. The smiles vanished. Heeding the advice of the
local Government Agency their parents had left town.
Poor Aunt Onecia had lain awake late into the night considering how she would explain to the boys that they
would be moving into her house. Both had such little experience of dealing with children as young as Malik and
Rashid.

"What have you done with Mum and Dad?" ques-
tioned Rashid looking at his Aunt directly. The boys listened intently as the tale unfolded, their parents had
gone away for a short while and had asked Aunt Onecia
and Uncle Tariq to take care of them but just along the
street and all their clothes and favorite toys would be
coming too, as if this suddenly made everything ok? The
boys remained unconvinced, their faces solemn, this had
not been the whole truth, but would have to suffice for
the moment.

Uncle Tariq remained silent scratching his head, it
was Malik who had reacted first, exploding like a fanta
bottle. Having worked himself into a boyish frenzy
shouting out "Where had they put his Mum and Dad?"
at the top of his voice followed by "I don't believe you!"
and with that he sprinted past them all pushing his way

through, out of the living room and out to his favorite place, the bottom of the garden.

Leaving Aunt Onecia and Uncle Tariq dumbstruck, now they were in a right quandary and what to do next? Malik headed down to his familiar back garden gate to check out the facts for himself. Puffing out his little chest, chuntering as he had looked in all their familiar hide and seek places. But to his utter dismay his Mum and Dad were nowhere to be seen.

"This was just a stupid joke and not funny anymore... MUM? DAD?" he shouted into the semi- darkness. Just silence as there was no one there to find. Refusing to go back inside, forty minutes had now passed as he hid outside behind the garden shed in total denial of the unfolding situation inside. In front of him he saw his old broken wooden seat waiting for disposal, he plonked himself down on it barely squeezing his rounded bottom between the arms of a battered frame, in a complete flummox.

With his arms firmly folded and bottom lip protruding, he tried to work out what he should do next; whilst still trying not to cry. Rashid had tried and failed to appease him, struggling to contain his own giant waves of childlike emotions. Their Aunt and Uncle showing themselves as inexperienced proxy parents who had landed the top job overnight, they had felt totally out of their depth. Unsure how to handle this rapidly escalating infantile situation. They had resorted to phoning other members of the family in hushed tones for advice but suddenly alienated, nobody had been available to answer their calls and that was how it would have to be for the next few weeks. They were on their own cast adrift in an open boat, making it up as they went along, in fact like most parents in the real world. Rashid mentioned to his Aunt about a little trick his mother had used in the past to tempt Malik back inside the house after an episode, with the mention of his favorite food. Normally a rumbling stomach would have worked, bringing the distressing scene swiftly to an end, but not tonight.

Despite encouraging noises and offers of bribery from his aunt, Malik flatly refused to come inside failing to understand why he felt so bereft, he simply wanted his Mum; he knew if he waited outside long enough, she would come back. Unfortunately, Uncle Tariq had not been physically strong enough to just pick him up and carry him inside. While Aunt Onecia had been keeping a beady eye on him through the kitchen window the sun had eventually dipped down behind the blackened sea far in the distance. Malik shivered and began to get a little chilled, his stomach growled more than once. Peering over the gate towards the sea he suddenly remembered he had a deep fear of the dark, so he would need to back down and head inside.

Creeping back along the edge of the wall and sneaking inside to the relative safety of his own little bed and his favorite cotton candy pillow. The significance of the strong fragrance of cotton candy would only become apparent to him in the following period of adjustment. Tomorrow, moving out day was going to be such a difficult day, as they had to pack up their belongings and move along the street to their Aunt and Uncle's bungalow. However tonight had been the last in his own house. It felt a little weird as his parents were not at home following their familiar bedtime routine, saying their goodnights and giving out warm hugs.

Aunt Onecia and Uncle Tariq hovered awkwardly at

the door not knowing what order things should be done, according to Rashid they had done everything the wrong way round and they quickly became reliant upon him for parenting guidance. The following day as promised by their Aunt and Uncle the boys realized everything was coming true. Their new home was far smaller with no familiar back garden that led down the path to the beach; now they had just a small backyard with a dirty patch of faded grass.

There were no more visible Dhow pirate ships sailing on the horizon for their fantasy adventures. Aunt Onecia only had a shabby looking shed in the backyard, Rashid aired his thoughts too holding his precious yellow ball under his arm, where would they play their games of football? They had no apparatus for climbing and no wooden swing hanging from the palm trees.

Malik reluctantly walked in through the front door of his new home, sniffing the air; his face scrunched up into a firm pout, clutching his little brown faded suitcase with his most important toys shut firmly inside. The other little hand holding tightly to the only constant in life, Rashid, who was still clutching his precious football to his chest. On the first night in the new house, they had followed the new instruction at bedtime; lights out early, and no night lights allowed. But Malik had a real fear of the dark, of course nobody would have known that except Rashid.

Lying motionless under the new quilt, surrounded by pitch blackness, Malik wept his salty tears silently into his favorite Mickey Mouse pillowcase, the familiar fragrance of Cotton Candy - his Mum's washing detergent gently reassuring him reminding him of home. Somehow, he thought he had managed to cry into his pillow without disturbing his brother but he could hear Rashid sniveling a little too and held out his hand in the dark to comfort him, grateful to feel another small hand enveloped in his own, they both promptly fell asleep.

The weekly fight with his Aunt to stop his pillowcase from being washed had become a part of his grieving process and had now escalated to become a tussle of wills. Who would win this battle as Malik started to hide it in some very strange places, such as under the bed, down in the garden shed, even in his little brown suitcase? It would not be until he reached adulthood that he would realize the relevance of this weekly saga. It had become his primary focus and imperative to him that the scent of the cotton candy washing detergent stayed the same as the day his mum had disappeared. He even convinced himself he could still smell it after several weeks and therefore it had to always remain the same unwashed scent. It had been all he had left of his mother to cling to, so by keeping it the same would make his Mum return, wasn't that how it worked the four-year-old convinced himself? This had been why he felt his aunt had failed to understand the importance of what he was saying, he had tried in vain to explain to her with his hands firmly on his hips, legs astride, wildly gesticulating with his arms but to no avail.

By week three he had drummed up a bit more self-confidence, readying himself for a full-on confrontation, spelling out his quandary in a rush and with some degree of wrath for someone so young. This time he firmly told his aunt he was leaving and needed to go home immediately, bravely explaining that her house smelt of lemon cleaner and his Mum's had always smelt of peanut butter cookies. He had even tried the age-old trick of "our

Mum is waiting for us back at home, so we have to leave now thank you for having us" with his suitcase packed up ready as a stunt making his way to the front door, but to no avail.

The doors had been securely locked to prevent any such escapees, even wimpish Uncle Tariq stood firm. The brothers had been entered into prearranged marriages with contracts cemented long before they had been born. Years later when the boys had reached their twenties, their parents returned from their Government Agency enforced exile.

On their return to Muscat, Leena and Jassim found their sons to be married and they had five grandchildren, three girls, two boys, and two daughters-in-law, the family had trebled in size. Malik married his childhood sweetheart Salma and Rashid had wed a beautiful model Thalia. They were all overjoyed on that day, simply glad to be a family again after being ripped apart. The cousins made the same sandcastles and pirate ships out of driftwood as their fathers had done before them. The long-awaited family reunion on their favorite beach with buckets of happy salty tears that gently flowed into the Arabian Sea and Dhows still sailed across the blue horizon.

Malik had given up on his childhood quest years ago to keep his pillow smelling of cotton candy fragrance hidden from his Aunt. But in the local supermarket he had tried to source the familiar detergent just in case! The stormy waters had subsided and all was calm.

The Honeysuckle Blossom

By Kathrin Spinnler

Their six-month wedding anniversary should have been perfect. It was one of those bright, sunny early-spring days when you can feel the world waking up from its frozen slumber. Jake headed home not long after lunch, looking forward to a weekend spent at home with his wife. In no great rush, he took a detour and wandered along a winding countryside road, through the woodlands at the edge of town. He slowed his steps and let the sunshine caress his face.

Once again, he marveled at the way luck had favored him. A beautiful wife, a cozy home and work he was passionate for – there was nothing more he could want. And yet, there was a niggle. Sometimes, he spotted tension in his wife Victoria's face. She'd lost weight in the past few weeks, pounds tumbling off her already-lean frame. Was there something bothering her that she couldn't tell him? Why wasn't she as happy as he was? As he stepped out of the forest, the breeze picked up, rustling the fresh springtime leaves.

A delicate fragrance tickled his nose and he stepped off the path to follow it. Set back from the path was a bush, dotted with spectacular white blooms, emitting a scent so intoxicating that a hundred bees buzzed around it. Jake cupped one of the flowers in his hand, waited for the bee to fly away, and drew it to his nose. 'Honeysuckle,' he recalled from a gardening magazine he'd perused.

'I never knew they smelled this way.' He'd considered buying them for the garden, but his plot was too sunny for the moisture-loving bush. He had to share this delight with Victoria. With a small tug, he pulled the bloom off the bush and took it home with him. The large cherry tree in front of his house was cloaked in early-spring leaves and small buds. Within weeks, it would be in full bloom, white and bridal-looking.

Victoria sat on the bench underneath it, waiting for him, as delicate and beautiful as the honeysuckle flower. With a sudden pang, he realized that she was also nearly as white. Was she ill? But she beamed up at him, smile turning into a giggle as he approached.

"Darling, what's that on your nose?" she asked.

"What?" He rubbed his nose and looked down at his yellow finger.

"Oh," he grinned. "Must have rubbed off from the flower." From behind his back, he pulled out the honeysuckle and handed it to her with a kiss. Beaming, she drew it to her nose. But as soon as she inhaled the fragrance, her face changed. Her fair eyes lost their focus and she stared into the distance.

"Everything all right, love?" Jake asked. But she didn't answer. Instead, a frown creased her forehead and she pursed her lips together. He didn't dare touch her, so he just stood there, watching as her fist closed around the flower, crushing it. The fragrance seeped through her fingers, stronger than ever.

"Honey, what is it?" he asked gently. Without answering, she sprung up, flung the bloom into the bushes, and ran into the house. Jake went after her, but by the time he reached the first floor, she'd already slammed shut the bedroom door. Victoria stayed in bed for the rest of the day, her small frame turned away from Jake. She wouldn't eat or drink. When he asked her what was wrong, her body trembled, but her lips remained sealed. After a lonely dinner, Jake got into bed beside her and drew her cold body towards him. He kissed her cheek and she snuggled up to him, face still turned away. "I'm sorry. Have I done something wrong?" he asked. She shook her head. "I thought you'd like the flower. It smelled so nice."

She sat up and turned around to face him. "Take me to it."

Jake frowned. "What do you mean?"

"The bush. I want to see it."

Jake brushed a strand of ebony hair from her cheek. "Okay. We can go tomorrow."

"No. Now." Her face was so determined that he didn't argue. Instead, he wrapped his wife in her warmest coat and winter scarf to protect her from the frosty night.

They stepped out into the darkness in silence, Jake's arm wrapped protectively around Victoria. The friendly cherry tree looked menacing in the dark, a looming shadow over the small cottage. Jake shuddered and turned back towards his wife, who trembled as an icy wind tugged at their silhouettes.

Finally, they arrived at the edge of the woodlands and Jake steered Victoria towards the bush. In the absence of the bees, the only sound was the wind, whispering through the branches. The fragrance was equally subdued, like an invisible, delicate cloud that hovered around the bush. As if entranced, Victoria stepped forward and held out her hand. She crouched down and touched one of the flowers. Drawing her nose down towards it, she inhaled deeply. Motionless, Jake watched his wife. He felt like a witness to a secret ritual, an almost shameful moment of privacy. But he didn't dare move away and disturb the scene enfolding in front of him. Victoria remained by the bush for what felt like an hour, eyes closed and inhaling the fragrance.

With a shudder, she got back up and turned to face Jake. "Let's go home." She took his hand and they walked back together, still not speaking.

Once they were home, Jake offered to make some tea. They sat in the kitchen, hands around their teacups, and gazed down at their drinks. After a moment, Victoria lifted her head and spoke. "We used to have a bush like that in our garden."

"What garden?"

"The one at our house ... before ..." She cast her eyes down. "Before I got taken away from my family."

Jake inhaled sharply and reached out a hand to touch hers. Victoria had been in an orphanage since she was six, and she'd always said she didn't remember her parents. All she'd been told by the matrons was that they had been drug addicts who couldn't look after her.

"When you gave me that flower, that scent, it brought it all flooding back," she said. "We had a bush like that in our yard. Whenever my father got violent, I'd cower in that bush, trying to block out the thumps, his yells, and my mother's screams. Today, when you came home with it, all the memories came flooding back ..."

A tear ran down her cheek. "I smelled the flower and suddenly, I was there again, pressing my hands over my ears and praying for it to all stop."

"Honey, I'm so sorry."

"No, don't be." She smiled through her tears. "You couldn't have known. Even I didn't remember any of it, not until today. For twenty-three years, I've wondered who I am and where I came from. I arrived at the orphanage without even a photograph to remember my family by. Now, at least I know." She paused and continued, more quietly. "Maybe it would have been better not to know."

They sat together for another while, then Jake stood up and stretched, ready to go to bed. Halfway up the stairs, he realized that Victoria wasn't behind him. She still sat at the table, motionless, and he returned to her side. Tears slid down her gaunt cheeks. He sat down and took her hands.

"There's something else, isn't there?" he murmured. She placed her head on his shoulder and sobbed.

"I'm just ... scared." Jake remained silent and waited for her to go on. "What if history repeats itself?"

He put an arm around her and kissed her cheek. "What do you mean?"

She shrugged his arm off and shot to her feet, turning to face him. But the sudden movement was too much for her. She swayed slightly, then crumpled on the floor before Jake could catch her.

"Victoria!" He screamed. At first, he thought she was unconscious, but she stirred faintly and then sat up and put her hand to her stomach.

"I'm okay, Jake, just got dizzy. I'm fine. More than fine, actually. I'm ..." Her quick downwards glance gave it away. A feeling of such intense joy swept through Jake's body that he could hardly catch his breath.

"Are you, really?" he whispered.

She gazed up at him, almost shyly. "I am."

He threw his arms around her and laughed out loud. But when he caught Victoria's expression, his smile faltered.

"But that's excellent news," he said. "It's what we've been waiting for, darling."

"Jake, what if history repeats itself?" She asked again. "What if the monster is in me, too? What if I'll turn out as violent as my father? I can't take the risk, I can't let the same happen to my ... my ... baby ..."

Her body convulsed with another round of sobs and Jake cradled her in his arms. "I know you, love. You're not a drug addict, and there's not a violent bone in your body. Not one, you hear me? And you forget that I'm here, too. No matter what happens, I will love this baby like I've never loved before." He touched her stomach. "I already do."

Her mouth twitched in a wan smile. "I do, too, but ..."

"And if anything were to happen, we're not alone. We can choose godparents, and then there's my sister, my parents. We're surrounded by people who would love to help our child." He paused to kiss away her tears. "Okay?"

Slowly, she nodded and relaxed into his embrace. For a long time, they sat on the floor and Jake held his wife and his unborn child. Their six-month wedding anniversary should have been perfect, but instead, it was so much more. It was the gateway to a whole new world for Jake and his budding family. He smiled as Victoria slowly slipped into sleep, and decided to bring home another flower tomorrow. Maybe a rose, or a lily, or a hyacinth. Just as long as it wasn't a honeysuckle blossom.

A Little Blob of Reminiscence

By Sohini Roy

January 7, 2021

Dear Diary,

I was wondering if you ever feel tired of me, imposing my meaningless thoughts on you, in black, bold letters. If you do, I'm sorry. As days are passing, I am understanding how it must feel. I try to spend each day at least a notch better than the previous, but somehow, I always go blank whenever I open you. Is it just me? .... I'm still trying to figure out why I live perpetually spaced out like this. So, will you bear with me? Just in case a good incident/ thought comes out someday? We can cherish it together! With every passing day, I'm growing more and more impatient. The world around me is in a big whirlpool, one I didn't want to be a part of (as you might've already figured out).

With each sunrise, my inner sun sets a little more. My spirits are tired of swimming upstream. I want to stop for a moment and go back. To the days when I could feel happiness without knowing it's meaning. When the flow of life was friendlier.... I remember, how these gusts of chilly winds, were once an opportunity to run around the park, feel the small sun within me, burn brighter than the galaxy. The park hasn't changed much, neither has my mind. But the circumstances and this body sure have. Now they're forcing this mind to fit into their narrow tunnel. I feel like that wooden flower-showpiece, Maa kept on trying to assemble. It fell apart from a new side each time. Should I give in too?

The temperature is dropping faster than my mood. I lock my phone and start off homewards. The winds are increasing their pace, almost mocking mine. Their touch cut through whatever little exposures they can find. I cringe and pull the coat from side to side, hoping to cover up a little more. Only the silver, soft moonlight seems unharmed by the blades of this winter. Among the whistle of winds and the rustle of the fallen leaves beneath my heavy boots, I hear a different sound. Perhaps I've stepped on something. A plastic container? I remove my right foot and squint, bending down a little bit. Colors? Are they? Not sure. I pick the box up: "Children's Watercolor Set (12 Shades)". Some child must've dropped it on the way. I can give it to the park's "Lost & Found" department tomorrow. Hope the child won't be too sad until then. Home is where the heart is. A cozy, warm haven to cherish. But what if the heart is dead and the cold radiates from within? I guess even the hearth cannot fix it.

But I don't want these thoughts to ruin whatever time is left until tomorrow morning; until the circus of life resumes. Without further ado, I head into the shower and let my worries trickle down, into the drain, with the warm water. It's weirdly pleasing to watch the little fronds dance as the water, splashing off my shoulders, nudge them invitingly. It's difficult to fix the distorted, metal tube. I know how heavy the boots are.

Shit! I just pressed out about two-thirds of the color!

Now a blob of cobalt blue sits authoritatively on my worn-out desk and the withered tube looks like it has been starved to death. Hmm...a hundred and fifty rupees....

Alright. I can afford a new one. Guess that's not too high a price for carelessness! Sorry, little one. Hope you haven't started associating much with your material possessions like every other grown-up. Yet. Ironically, it's been a few months since I've painted, out of a conscious will. The blob of paint seems like a Siren's call. I let go of my doubts and surrender to it. But what should I paint?

The sweet smell of paint takes me back to the rough, cemented floor of the old kitchen at the back. A plump, little child sat there, crayons spread all around her, weaving her dreams onto blank white pages. Her hand knew no boundaries. The crayons sometimes escaped the paper and continued on the textured floor like the pen of a seismograph.

A small scolding came from the other end, where Grandma was cooking yet another delicious recipe, sitting on the new, red stool. The little girl was so proud that none of the neighbors can have the dishes she could, because, only Grandma cooked like that. And Grandma was hers. She ran over to the old, wrinkled woman, clad in a serene, white saree, that was softer than rose petals. Her nostrils had been triggered by the aroma of fried potatoes, sizzling away in the grey kadhaai. She knew Grandma would soon be tasting it to check the seasoning.

That's it! Maybe I should capture these precious memories! 'Coz why not? My mind is holding hands with the old, maroon brush, in between my fingers. Nothing can interrupt their association, now. The full-moon inside this dark mind is pulling the tides higher and higher. Soon, light and dark shades of blue bring back the thousand different fragrances that were kept hidden in the depths of my sub-conscience.

9o'clock. The most crucial time of weekday mornings. The world tried to rush by and the rush, in turn, stagnated them at every corner of the street. Office time, as we called it there.

The streets of Calcutta mimicked fishing nets at that hour. Cars ran from everywhere to everywhere and the person who was the most stressed out about being late, was the catch of the day. Oblivious of the turbulence, the little girl fished out the most fascinating thing in Maa's purse. A pale, red lipstick. Just a stroke of it could turn you into an adult. But Maa always stopped her from growing up so fast. She reasoned out that her lips would also darken up like Maa. But she wasn't a baby! She knew it'd make her look like those pretty aunties from the serials Grandma watched! While Maa was busy wiping off the excess vermillion from her forehead, she sneakily pouted her lips and voila! You wouldn't find her until Maa had left. When the suspicions had subsided, she would quietly grab the pink scarf. It's just the perfect saree for her.

Standing in front of the mirror, she would gauge the accuracy of her look. Pretty precise! To her veiled eyes, the world was bright and pink. The deeper the blue, the stronger the sickly-sweet smell, of age-old, cheap cosmetics. How am I smelling it for real?! It must be a dream. I shut the thoughts and enjoy this unexpected escape. At least it's a happy one. The rich aroma of ghee and freshly baked cookies! Her feet had followed the trail her nose had discovered. CookieMan! Until that moment, she had always known JimJam was the best. To her, it was the expensive perfume that South City Mall applied each day before welcoming guests.

Those days she could help herself to a cup of instant coffee, back home. But the coffee from the café was always creamier. However much she tried, the consistency was never perfect back in her kitchen. From the price tags attached to the cookie trays, she knew, Maa would get her one each of the two bestsellers. So, she took the seat closest to the counter. She shouldn't miss out on the little pieces they offered for tasting. But she was disappointed that the rich aroma wasn't there anymore. Not as much as at the entrance. Later, Maa compensated for that with a small bag of mixed cookies.

Now her home, too, was adorned with the same aromatic perfume. Reading is a good habit. But there's nothing that ever called out to her thousand years old, teenage soul. Well, okay, maybe a couple of Ruskin Bond books? But, that's it. Shalini completed the entire "Nancy Drew" series, right in front of her eyes. She was one crazy reader! The library always smelled so good. But she never figured out what the smell really was. Every "library class" she issued a book (because she had to) and dropped it back on the shelf, by the next. When half of the class was so hyped up about Percy Jackson, she finally knew the school library was actually possessed by the nostalgic smell of old and new books. That was probably the gentlest expression of the powerful peer pressure. Indeed, she was lucky. Indian childhoods are shrouded in the smell of Dettol. It is, in a way, the smell of India. Back in the schooldays, once, while talking about our favorite smells of day-to-day stuff, the most common ones turned out to be LPG, petrol, bleaching powder, kerosene, the Bengal Chemical phenyl, peach and strawberry flavored lip balms, old books and coffee.

When I was done mentioning mine, the whole room literally freaked out, "You don't like the smell of Dettol?!"

"Oh! Yeah! And Dettol..." There's no question of disliking it! We, sure, were a bunch of weirdos! But the question is: How will my brush, bring back my memories with the ineffable smell of the orange-brown liquid, in the green-lidded bottle, here, on this paper? Perhaps this one can't be justified just with colors. For the first time in a couple of years, time seems to be on my side. The cookies, the lipstick, my Grandma, cannot be freed from the rusted chains of time. But the chemist's, two blocks away, pack up at eleven. It's just nine now. I grab my purse and the faded sweater, from the edge of the wrinkled bedsheet. I hope it isn't too obvious that I am in my pajamas. Not that I care, anyway... The tall guy at the counter was looking quite confused. I bet he hasn't seen someone so happy, to buy a glass bottle full of antiseptic liquid, ever before! I just can't stop giggling while breaking the seal. The mouth of the bottle is magnetically pulled by my nose.

Within the fraction of a second, the sweet smell of my childhood, the smell of the little blankets, Grandma stitched for me, drying in the summer sun; the smell of the soft, caring hands cleaning the wounds on my knees; the ivory chamber where the sky-blue attired nurse, with an everlasting furrowed brow at the bridge of her beak nose, getting ready to vaccinate me; Mama, cleaning the generations old, red and blue, rubber cloth, my baby sister had messed up, her innocent smile defying her father's cowered nose; and a younger me, laughing my lungs out at them.... gush down my soul breaking through the age-old accumulations of regrets and bitterness; loneliness.

Underneath the starry, winter, night sky, I can feel the corner of my lips reminiscing their lost habit of touching the reddened ears; the brows tired from furrowing day after day, moving apart happily; the eyes finally remembering how it felt to cringe in unconditioned happiness... it's the fragrance of warmth. Only a part of my rationality is busy, trying to understand how the colorful pieces of paper, with acquired values and importance, could never bring the same level of ecstasy, as this little sea of brown wonder. As this ocean of unforgettable memories.

Riya and her ghosts

By Ananya Madhu

The thumping had started right when Riya decided to paint. She hated it when Mr. Nath was in his I-hate-the-world mood. He got riled up about anything as trivial as a bird flapping its wings 'loudly' outside his window. She set the paintbrush down and got up from her seat at the dinner table and made her way up the stairs to see what had gotten Mr. Nath in this mood. As expected, it was a bird. Just a calm crow perched at the windowsill.

"That vicious bird is disturbing my morning yoga session." Mr. Nath said it with so much venom that only a ninety-year-old ghost could. This was a first - not the venomous remark but the yoga session. Why did a ghost have to do yoga anyway?

"You never did yoga before, have you Mr. Nath?" Riya went to the window and shooed the bird away before things got bad.

"When I was alive, I was a yoga instructor." He said vehemently.

Just as Riya was about to give a sarcastic reply, Anita Aunty glided in through the wall. "Oh dear, I thought someone had kidnapped you. I saw your paintbrush lying on the paper like it was thrown there. So, I thought- oh god- you scared me...you-" For a ghost, Anita Aunty panted too much.

"Why would you think someone would kidnap me?" Riya asked a little skeptically. A look was shared between Mr. Nath and Anita Aunty that she couldn't decipher.

"Nothing, my dear. Have your breakfast." With that Anita Aunty dragged her to the dining room.

Riya was ten years old and lived in a cabin in the woods with five ghosts. She didn't find it odd or scary to live with them. Kids are always told to be scared of ghosts. If they are never told to be scared of them why would they ever be? They were her family. Everyone dotted on her like she was their own child. No one knew where she came from. She was found at their doorstep ten years ago, wrapped in a white cloth with nothing but a note that said 'Sorry Riya'.

There had been many debates the following week as to what to do with this baby. Anita Aunty and Sarah, a thirty-year-old ex-teacher was enthralled with the idea of growing a baby. Vijay, a farmer who had lost his life in a flood few years ago, and Damini Bai, who died under mysterious circumstances, weren't too happy with the prospect of growing a child. But it was Mr. Nath who came up with the conclusion that the baby, Riya would be taken care of by them until she had come of age. They would cook and take care of all her needs.

Ghosts had an advantage of stealing things without ever being caught. They didn't know exactly when all of this would have to stop. No one asked Mr. Nath when she would come of age and after few years of taking care of her, no one wanted to know. They didn't want her to go. But they knew she would have to. This wasn't the life she deserved. There were times when humans wandered into the cabin. The five of them made sure to scare them away. Riya was kept hidden from the world but she was growing up and she had started wandering on her own.

One day Mr. Nath had found her playing with a man outside the cabin. Enraged, he scared the man senseless and scolded Riya till Anita Aunty stepped in to stop him. It was decided then that Riya would never go out of the cabin unaccompanied. She was also home schooled by Sarah. The ghosts didn't keep the knowledge of the living world hidden from Riya. They explained to her the abnormality of her family. Riya didn't mind it one bit. She loved her family despite its shortcomings. And they loved her immensely. Riya was served paneer makhni and roti for breakfast. Sarah had joined her at the dinner table to ask her questions about yesterday's class. Riya answered all of it.

After breakfast Riya had her usual class up to noon. While she was eating her lunch all the ghosts, except for Anita Aunty who was with Riya, gathered at Mr. Nath's reading room to discuss about her.

"She is ten years old. Don't you think we have to send her to the outside world?" Sarah asked Mr. Nath. Vijay nodded his head approvingly.

"I agree with Sarah. She needs better schooling. I don't mean to say Sarah is unqualified." He looked at her apologetically.

"Vijay Bhai, I do agree with you. Riya can't stay here forever learning from me. I've been dead for quite a long time. There's so much that has changed since then. Riya is very smart. A child like her, needs better education. Besides, she needs people in her life who are living not dead." Sarah spoke fervently.

"So, what do you suggest Sarah? We'll just send her somewhere?" Mr. Nath was riled up.

Just when Sarah was about to reply Anita Aunty popped into the room. "She's gone. Riya is gone. Someone kidnapped her. I- I." Anita Aunty was gasping for air.

"Anita Masi, calm down. Now tell me where did you last see Riya?" Sarah asked her steadily. All of them knew that when Anita Aunty got jittery others should remain calm.

"She was eating her lunch. I was in the kitchen making desert for her. When I came back, Riya wasn't at the dinner table nor was her plate."

"So, the kidnapper took the plate along with her. Must have been a hungry kidnapper." Vijay said amusingly. Sarah gave him a pointed look.

"Masi, she must have gone outside. Did you check around the house?" Sarah asked Anita Aunty gently. Just then they heard a laugh. It was undoubtedly Riya's laughter. They heard another voice too. They floated towards it. Riya was sitting on the staircase with a girl who looked just about her age. Her plate was on the ground. They were both looking at something in Riya's cupped palm. Riya could feel their presence whenever they were near her, so she turned around to look at them. She had the widest grin on her face. When the other girl turned around to look at them, they vanished.

"Anita Aunty, where are you? Where did you all go? Look what I found- a ladybird!" Riya looked around to see any signs of their presence even though she couldn't feel it.

"Who are you talking to?" asked the other girl whose name was Kyra. "I-um." Riya thought about the absurdity of her life and replied animatedly "Oh, no one. Let's play!" with that both the girls ran out to play.

The Ghosts watched Riya play with her new friend. She seemed so happy and at ease. They decided not to interrupt. This went on for weeks. Mr. Nath found it very comforting to know that Riya had found a human friend.

"She looks so happy." Anita Aunty observed solemnly.

It didn't go unnoticed by Mr. Nath. "Why do you sound sad, Anita?" He inquired.

"It's just that seeing her play with that girl made me realize how much she's missing out on. We should have done something about her when we found her at our doorstep. We stole her childhood. We – we really- we." She burst out crying. Mr. Nath clucked. Tears made him queasy. So, he awkwardly patted her back.

Suddenly Anita Aunty straightened herself and glided out of the room. Mr. Nath sighed and went back to reading his book. As days passed by, Riya and Kyra became best friends. Seeing this bond between them, Anita Aunty started planning something. She decided to pay Kyra's family a visit.

Kyra lived on the outskirts of the forest. She was an only child. Her mom and dad, Pihu and Karan Ashok were teachers. Anita Aunty started picturing Riya living among them as their daughter. She saw her growing up to be a very successful person. Saw all the things she would get from this life. She knew what she had to do. Ghosts were considered as malicious haunters. Anita Aunty decided to haunt this family but not maliciously. She decided to slip into their dreams and leave tidbits of Riya's images. This went on for a week.

The Ashoks talked about the recurring images of the same girl in both of their dreams. They were spooked but they felt a need to go looking for this girl. One day some force made them follow their daughter and were shocked to see her go into the forest. They ran after Kyra, calling her name. They stopped dead on their tracks when they saw the little girl that visited them in their dreams. They felt a sudden compulsion to take her back home and care for her like their own. All the ghosts other than Anita Aunty were appalled by the site of two grown humans. They decided to scare them away but Anita Aunty stopped them. She confessed them of her endeavors. They were stunned. Not for long.

They understood the hidden motive behind her actions. Miss Sarah was rather impressed by her. Anita Aunty decided to reveal her ultimate plan before they all got excited.

"We have to erase ourselves completely from Riya's life." She said it quickly. All were quiet for some time. Damini Bai and Vijay were the first ones to accept this. Sara acquiesced in her decision. Now it was up to Mr. Nath for the final decision. He looked at Riya and, after thirty years since his death, he cried. There was dead silence except for Mr. Nath's sobs. Everyone waited for him to calm down and he did at last.

"Do it, Anita." And with that he left. Anita Aunty went to Riya. She had frozen all of them in their places when she saw the Ashoks. She took a deep breath and entered Riya's head. She altered her memories. And then the Ashoks. It was tiring but she didn't stop. Then she made them all walk to their home. None of the ghosts got to say goodbye to Riya. Anita was depleted of her energy. She felt herself evanesce. Just then she felt a surge of energy run through her. Mr. Nath. She looked at him and smiled. Both of them changed the whole truth of Riya's life and gave her a fictitious one that was much normal than her actual truth.

Finally, she snapped the link connecting her to Riya and the Ashoks. And Riya finally became part of that family like it was how it always had been. Now there was no one left who knew these ghosts. They didn't know this but they would remain in the back of Riya's mind slowly fading away like the fragrance of a wilted flower.

"There's a loophole in this." Damini said. "What about the people who know the Ashoks?"

"We need more energy for changing their truths. I don't think-" Anita was interrupted by Sarah.

"What are we here for then?" she smiled at her. That day all the ghosts of the cabin changed the truths of all the people who knew the Ashoks. As their end neared, they had a smile on their faces drawn there by the memories of Riya that flitted across their minds. They crossed over at last. They were proud to know that they had once been Riya's Ghosts. In a way, they still were.

The Fragrant Embrace of Jasmine

By Linda Hibbin

G wen needed her mum. She found comfort in her presence as she listened to the consultant, not really hearing what he was saying. Later she wept into her mother's softness soothed by the familiar fragrance which brought back memories of childhood cuddles. Made the world feel a safe place. Dispelled the monsters of dreams and banished fear. Suddenly, Gwen's eyes lit up.

'Do you remember waiting outside Woolies, pretending you didn't know why we were really there?' She wiped her eyes and blew her nose. Conjured a small smile from nowhere. 'You always gave me a sixpenny piece and told me to go and buy my own Pick 'n Mix. She got up, went into the kitchen and filled the kettle, continuing the conversation. 'I'll take the sound and bounce of the wooden floorboards to my grave.'

Gwen laughed, remembering herself as a child. 'A visit to Woolworths was on a par with a trip to Santa's Grotto. No, it was better. A wonderland for children. So many toys, books, art stuff, cheap jewelry, hair ribbons and tortoiseshell hair slides. Not real tortoiseshell, of course.' While she waited for the kettle to boil, Gwen stared out the window.

The squirrels were active, the youngsters learning fast. They leapt from branch to branch, sometimes misjudging the strength of springy twigs. They'd fall to the ground where they seemed to bounce like rubber balls. The antics of the creatures provided hours of entertainment, especially for the dog, Poppy, who sat at the window smearing the glass with her wet nose. Making the coffee, Gwen's memories returned to Woolworths. So many shop counters with eye catching displays, but it was the cosmetics counter she always made a beeline for.

'The cosmetic counter seemed to stretch for miles. It was an island ruled by white coated assistants standing in the middle. To me they were like film stars with their bright red lipstick and painted nails. Thinking back, they could have been teenagers. They seemed old. Everyone's old when you're a child. 'Oh, there were hundreds of things to see. It smelled like a cottage garden. Talc, shampoos, soaps, creams, lipsticks, face powders, eye shadows, lotions full of promise. There I'd stand clutching my pocket money, peering over the edge of the counter looking for the blue box.'

'Soir de Paris.' Gwen rolled the musical words around her tongue. She shrugged theatrically and tried to sound French.

'Evening in Paris.'

'I'd point to it and exchange my five shillings for your birthday present. Five shillings, mum! Twenty-five pence! I even got a few pennies change! We're talking about pre-decimal currency. Those were the days, eh?'

Were there any biscuits in the tin or had she polished them off last night? 'I'd tuck the paper bag in my pocket and then dash to the Pick 'n Mix near the front of the shop. I bet it was strategically placed so that the sweetness filtered out of the doors as people came and went. Got the taste buds of passers-by going!'

Gwen's taste buds were dancing! Her mouth had the audacity to water with the memory! She paused. Glanced out of the window, not seeing the squirrels. Remembering.

'The fragrance of Pick 'n Mix was as enticing as your perfume, mum,' she murmured.

Gwen carried the coffee and biscuits into the living room. The choice was mind blowing. It was surprising how many sweets you could buy for six pence. Four ounces! A paper bag of heaven. God! Think of all those E numbers and artificial colorings. I bought a few retro sweets not long ago. They just didn't have the same kick. Especially the sweet tobacco!

'I can't remember what I liked most, but once a week, on my way home from school as a teenager, I bought a quarter of coffee creams. Purple wrappers, or were they blue? Do you remember me twisting the empty wrappers into wine glasses, and lining them up like soldiers?'

She dunked a biscuit. 'Still my favorite but harder to come by.'

Yes, it was a tragedy when Woolies shut its doors for ever. 'When I went to bed, I'd look at the blue box, tightly wrapped with crisp cellophane. The Parisian skyline and the Eiffel Tower were silhouetted faintly against midnight blue. The silver words, 'Soir de Paris,' stood out loud and clear.

Years later, at art school, I realized the design was Art

Deco.' Gwen sighed.

'The box was beautiful. It seemed so luxurious and I knew you didn't have many luxuries.' She gave a smidgen of biscuit to the dog.

'Do you remember showing me the Evening in Paris box dad gave you during the war? It said it was temporary 'Victory' packaging, but the contents were unchanged. What happened to it, mum? I'm surprised I never found it. Must have been special, for you to keep it.'

She sipped her coffee as her thoughts meandered back over the years. 'I kept the gift wrapping and used it each year. You always unwrapped the present so carefully. You didn't seem to notice when I sneaked the wrapping away, hid it in my bedroom for the next birthday. I was learning to recycle, even then.' Gwen grinned.

'I know. You don't have to tell me. You turned your back deliberately to give me time to stow the wrapping paper away. It's funny, isn't it? All mothers act the innocent for their kids.' She nibbled a biscuit.

'We deserve awards for our acting skills. I didn't sense anything out of the ordinary as a child.' She wagged her finger. 'You were very convincing, especially when you were so excited when you opened the present. "Oh!" you'd cry, "what a lovely surprise, Pet!"' Gwen inhaled, adjusted the scarf draped around her shoulders.

'I can still smell the perfume, mum. Faintly. A sweetness of jasmine and violets. The scent of the jasmine I planted in the garden always takes me back to those times. Years later I identified the underlying fragrance I didn't recognize as a child. Vanilla and sandalwood.'

She closed her eyes, breathed in. Said quietly, 'Did you know jasmine means motherhood?' Poppy jumped onto the sofa and settled down, chin on Gwen's lap. Gwen shivered and leaning forward, pulled the scarf up around her neck. 'Did you actually use all the perfume between birthdays, or did you collect a stash of it?' The dog turned over, legs in the air, begging for a tummy rub. Gwen was thinking about the perfume bottle.

In her mind's eye she watched her mother gently unpeel the cellophane, open the lid and slide the glass perfume bottle out of the box. To the child, it was a cobalt blue jewel. It was the same ritual each year. Her mother gently twisted off the silver top and carefully, with her fingernail, prised the tiny, black rubber plug from the bottle. Next, she slowly waved the bottle under her nose, eyes closed, inhaling the fragrance, like a connoisseur evaluating a wine. Finally, she put her finger over the open bottle, tipped it and dabbed her perfumed finger behind her ears, on each wrist and the base of her throat.

Gwen stroked her own throat. The dog still waited patiently for her tummy rub. Cards! Gwen always made her mum a card to accompany the present and it stayed on the mantelpiece for weeks. Some had been more successful than others. 'Do you remember the perfume bottle card, mum? I cut out the shape of the bottle and filled the space with overlapping pieces of blue tissue. Different shades of blue. I was so proud of it. And, oh my god, the disaster doggy? Who could forget that? I tried making the dog pop out when the card was opened, but it dropped out! I was mortified but you laughed and told me not to be a soppy date. You made a paste with flour and water, stuck the dog in the card and waved it over the gas stove until it dried and stuck.' Gwen nodded her head. 'If I remember right that card stayed on the mantelpiece until Christmas!'

Gwen buried her nose in the woolly scarf around her

neck. Her breath warmed the fibers. It was a comforting cushion. Eyes closed, she covered her face with the scarf, seeing her mother on the field, the dogs frolicking around her, the scarf wrapped around her head and neck. She felt a familiar calmness, a reassurance and deep love, seep into her flesh, her mind, her soul. Lowering the scarf, Gwen caressed the empty perfume bottle with the cracked, silver top. Spent a few moments in thought.

'Time to put you away, mum,' she said sadly, carefully placing the bottle and scarf into a plastic bag. She sucked the air out of the bag with a straw and sealed it to preserve the essence of her mother.

As always, at times when Gwen needed her mum and unwrapped the precious keepsakes, the ghost of the fragrance of a woman long gone, dispelled the monsters of dreams and banished all fear. 'I have missed you, mum. Thank you for being with me today.' She clutched the bag to her chest. 'See you soon.'

Nosy

By Udita Mukherjee

He had always been a bit of a loner. The reason was simple enough and hardly in his control. You see, he had been born without a nose. As a young boy, growing up in a time when Ramayana blared through the television screens every evening like clockwork, like a ritual, his classmates didn't even give him a chance. Surpanakha, they would tease as he walked down the corridor. The adults seemed to like him. Why wouldn't they? He ate his green vegetables without fuss, swallowed the stinkiest fish without complaint. They say half the taste is in the smell, lucky for him, he could eat healthier than other kids his age. This definitely did not help his popularity.

Middle school started, kids started showing signs of maturity, they outgrew Ramayana and in turn, Surpanakha. Things were looking up for him when suddenly a small boy with round glasses and a lightning-shaped scar took the world by storm. Whilst others took refuge in the magical world of the books, he found himself under attack because of it. People around him found an escape from the harsh realities of life through the books even as he found himself imprisoned in his personal hell due to them. Voldemort, his classmates screeched at him, as if the character was created especially for this, to taunt him. The adults seemed to like him still. Why wouldn't they?

Whilst others his age rolled around in mud, he took special care to stay clean. He had to, he couldn't risk getting dirty because that led to smelling bad. No one would tell him he smelt bad, he would never be able to tell himself, which would only lead to more jokes at his expense. He couldn't afford that. High school started. People busied themselves in dating boys and girls. No one gave him the time of day. Occasionally, he would hear whispers of You-Know-Who or He Who Must Not Be Named going around and realize they were talking about him. Just within earshot, so they could watch him squirm in discomfort. He felt as alienated as ever. The adults still liked him.

Or did they? They just pitied him, always had apparently, he had just been too innocent to see it for what it was. The poor boy, look at his poor face, see how he has no friends, they said when they thought he couldn't hear them. The children were better in this respect, at least they were honest and upfront about it. Isolated from his species, he found he had a lot of free time. He devoted it all to academics, he found it to be a solitary pursuit, soothing by its very nature. The adults tolerated him. Why wouldn't they? He got good grades and always did his homework. Oh, how his classmates detested him.

He got into a good college. College people are more accepting he had heard but his life had taught him the hard way to never have any expectations. So he didn't. It was an awkward age. He was an adult now, as were other people his age, like his classmates.

Oh, the suspense! Would they call him names or detest him or manage to tolerate him? It had to be one of the three. Instead, it took an entirely different direction. They ignored him. They just didn't seem to care. College people can be pretty apathetic when they want to. How cool! He carried on as before, studying, bathing and eating healthy. While that doesn't sound like a lot, try thinking of one person you can say the same about.

You'll probably come up blank. If you're lucky you get one or two out of these three things from the people you surround yourself with. I, myself check one and a half out of three, I study and eat. Anyway, here was a potential role model for humanity, a poster child, unsung and unseen, going quietly about his life, ignored by his kind. He didn't seem to mind though; school had ensured he would be dead on the inside. He found himself at the start of a very promising career. He had studied to become a surgeon. A very well thought out decision on his part, he believed. The smell of blood or exposed organs or gastrointestinal fluids or any other disgusting human body bit really, had no effect upon him. He had never felt woozy or faint at the sight of flesh being cut open, right from the very beginning. All thanks to his nose, or lack thereof.

There was another reason behind his career choice. The mask. Maybe if his face remained hidden from his colleagues, he would finally have someone to talk to. With the mask on, he looked just like every other person. He had forgotten one tiny detail. The masks had to come off eventually. People did leave the operating theatres at one point or another.

While the nurses and doctors respected him alike, they couldn't maintain eye contact with him. It was just another form of being ignored. He had gotten used to it by now. He couldn't complain, the nurses obeyed him and the doctors listened to him. They sought his advice too. Why wouldn't they? He was the best in his field. However, he would have liked for them to ask about his opinions, outside of work. He knew they never would though, those things require eye contact. He resigned himself to his fate, spending his life as a pariah. The pandemic hit. While he would have coped with its accompanying solitude better than most people, his line of work meant he would never know this for sure. The profession called for all hands on deck every day. He gave it his all. He had replaced studying with his work, all his time was devoted to it.

There would be days when he would get only twenty minutes of sleep. However, he had never complained about anything and he wasn't about to start now. The patients admired him. Why wouldn't they? They had never come across someone as dedicated as this man.

One day, in the middle of the lockdown, the hospital got a new patient. She wasn't the only one admitted that day but she was the only seventy-five-year-old. She had come in for a simple surgery with almost zero risk but then she tested positive. She was kept under observation for a few days as operating in her condition could prove to be fatal. When he was finally brought in for a consultation, he took one look at her and knew she would die. There was no way they could carry out the procedure, it would only accelerate the inevitable. His colleagues knew this, he knew they knew. However, no one could break this news to the seventy-five-year-old. So instead, he decided to distract her every time he made his rounds.

"What did you have for breakfast today?"

"Have you pooped?"

"What do you think of Nurse S?"

"Is your urine pale yellow or sunflower yellow?"

"I heard your favorite TV show was particularly trying today. Tell me what happened."

She always played along. She knew what was in store for her. She wasn't dumb. However, she was funny and colorful. She had decided to stay that way till the end.

"I had ice-cream sundae for breakfast."

"I pooped out the entire sundae from yesterday in swirls."

"She is particularly anal about my medicines."

"My urine was lavender today actually, should I be concerned?"

"Well, if you expect me to bare my soul to you like that, at least show me your face first."

"Your soul was hidden in your favorite TV show all this while? No wonder I couldn't find it in all these reports," he responded, shuffling the files he was holding.

"Stop buying time. You're wearing a PPE suit already, take off your mask, you'll be fine. I want to see the face of my new best friend." He felt something stir inside him when he heard that last part. It was what he had always wanted, someone to talk to. So, he took off his mask and prepared for the worst, put up a mental wall to bang his head against at the disappointment he knew was about to follow. But she just laughed and he was at a loss for words.

"Well, aren't you very nosy for someone with your facial structure?" She guffawed. That was a brilliant pun, it demanded laughter. He gave in, he laughed with her.

"Asking me what color I peed in the cheek," she shook her head.

Other people had laughed at him but this was different. It felt different. She wasn't laughing at his expense, she was laughing with him, like friends do after teasing you out of love. He loved the feeling, it was new and warm. For the rest of her not-very-long life, she said he had to bare his soul to her. It was his turn, after all he knew her digestive system in detail and where her soul resided, it would only be fair. So he did.

Why wouldn't he? She was his best friend. He told her about his life, about the people his age both when he was a child and when he became an adult.

"Well, they were absolute pieces of shit! Thank the Lord you don't have a nose, shit smells shitty, you know? Be glad you never had to smell the shits around you." He laughed so hard she swore she heard him snort.

"Shit smells shitty? Please tell me more!" He managed to say between the laughs.

"Well, rope smells like sand in your shoes. Paper smells like silk in your hand. Roses smell like pastel shades. Coffee smells like water splashing your face. You smell clean. I smell like a meadow. Petrol smells like a toothache that is comforting to press against. Autumn smells like a scab you like to worry. Chocolate smells like a hug from your best friend. Those are the important things, everything else is just a distraction."

"Rope made the cut but fire didn't, I am a little bit concerned."

"Fire smells like the smoke in your eyes, how is that not obvious?"

"You're right, my mistake," he smiled.

She showed him a new world. She taught him how to smell. She gave him reasons to live and then she passed away, as quietly as he had lived. He was there when she took her last breath, holding his hand.

In that moment, he smelt tall trees, flowers, green grass, flowing water, chirping birds, he smelt the fragrance of an entire meadow.

Jasmine

By Cara Finegan

I was standing outside Lidl, two meters away from the masked person in front of me, when the smell of jasmine wafted into my nostrils. I turned my head left, then right trying to sniff where it came from. I glanced along the queue, it snaked right along the shopfront and around the corner. People standing on markers, scrolling through their phones, making small talk with those around them. Again. Just a whisper of a scent. That nostalgic torment of remembrance that makes you smile before reality knocks you to the ground.

I tilted my head catching it on the breeze. I breathed it in and was transported back to Port El Kantaoui. My honeymoon. That magical first trip away from home. Two weeks. Just me and him. Our first time spent together. Living, breathing, sleeping, and looking after each other. No family, no friends. Tunisia of all places. A beautiful, tragic dichotomy. Arid, poverty ridden deserts and lush jasmine filled hotel gardens. Whose marble floors and walls and ceilings made the shacks and hungry children disappear. It's funny how easily blindness materializes when we're distracted by ornate facades. The pretense that something doesn't exist because we hide our faces or stick our fingers in our ears la-la-la-ing. Children selling bundles of the jasmine flower tied with twine, the fragrance lulling us into lovelorn scenarios and romantic trysts. I kept the bundle of jasmine that he bought me. It stayed by my bedside for almost fifteen years. That trip was my "sprinkling".

All the inklings I had that things weren't as they should be. The many persistent little nudges that I sensed, then shook away. The feelings of "off-ness". I should have listened. I didn't. I was in love. "Love is blind" people say. They're wrong. It's blind, deaf, dumb... and dumber.

My first red flag was waved gaily in my face when he told me that I wasn't allowed to phone home to tell mum that we had arrived safely.

It was 1997, mobiles weren't common then.

"We're on our honeymoon for Christ sake."

"I told Mum I'd let her know that we arrived safely."

"You're going to send her a postcard, aren't you?"

"Yes. But that'll take days."

"So, you're not happy enough being here with me. Your husband."

I threw my arms round him, kissed his face.

"Course I am. I'm sorry." The first of many apologies.

"Sometimes you're so selfish." He pushed me away.

I felt guilty, disgusted at myself. "I don't mean to be."

I bought a postcard. He posted it on his way to the pool. It never did arrive. Some of my jasmine-scented honeymoon was beautiful – evening walks on the beach, watching sunsets, drinking wine at the edge of the lapping ocean, and taking photos. But the blissfully romantic periods were peppered with moments of confusion and doubt. The night he bought me the jasmine he locked my purse in a safe and wouldn't let me take it out in case I bought something frivolous in the souvenir shops.

Our spending money was to be used on us alone. It was our honeymoon after all. He gave me the silent treatment when I cried with frustration and begged for just a little bit of money to buy mum a scarf. He made me feel childish and stupid for doubting his good sense. We left for dinner, his arm around my shoulder, smelling my hair, kissing my head. A street child selling jasmine danced along beside us and he bought two bundles. He handed a bundle to me.

"What's your name wee man?"

"Youssef. Your wife is very beautiful Mr."

"She's not too bad. She'll do. For now." He winked at the child.

"Very beautiful Mr." I smiled and sniffed my jasmine.

"Isn't she lucky to have me?" We found a restaurant along the marina.

And the sound of the sea and the twinkle of the stars helped me forget. At the bar he laughed and chatted with the pretty waitress as he settled our bill. He gave her a large tip and a bundle of jasmine. Touching the flower to his nose first.

"Beautiful flowers for an exquisite woman." He bowed.

The waitress blushed. I turned away, looking out to the moon on the horizon and listening to the waves finding the shore. I swallowed down a lump in my throat. On our walk back to the hotel I didn't kill the mood. I smiled and pushed annoyances from my head. If he noticed that I was quiet, he didn't say.

"Do you want to move on there, love?"

The deep voice of the man behind me in my Lidl line

brought me back. I checked to see how close I was getting to the door and wondered where the pretty waitress was now. The woman who received flowers from my husband on my honeymoon. A man behind me in the line tutted loudly.

"How long do you think this shit's going to go on for?"

"God, I don't know." I replied.

"But at least the weather has been gorgeous. We've been very lucky."

"Thank God for small mercies."

"You're right there."

"Do you think it's true what they're saying?"

"What's that then?"

"That it's all only happening so that they can distract us from that aul 5G?" I laughed at him.

"Sure, who's to know." I didn't believe that at all.

"Let's just wash our hands, social distance and hope for the best, eh?"

"Aye. I suppose." I took another two-meter saunter to the next marker.

There it was again. Jasmine. It's funny how I could never remember the good parts of our honeymoon. It was the day before we left Port El Kantaoui for home. He had planned an excursion for us. Jeeps through the desert to a remote village where pottery was made and then finished off with a boat trip and dinner. It was to be around 36° that day.

After breakfast, while he was throwing things into a rucksack, I went out to take pictures from the balcony. It was our last day and our corner room balcony looked out onto the quiet gardens of the hotel, it got the sun all day long. I wanted to capture the view from our honeymoon suite so that we would have the picture forever. I remember what I was wearing that day - a black bikini top and a pair of white cotton hot pants. My bundle of jasmine in my hand. I was only taking pictures for a minute but when I turned to go in, the balcony door was locked, the room empty. I called for him, knocked the window, I tried to wiggle the lock. He had already left.

At first, I thought it was a joke, I soon realized that he wasn't coming back. The rucksack with towels, sun cream and snacks were gone. The hours that last day crawled past so slowly, the searing sun beat down on my not-yet-sun-creamed -up skin. I waited for the cleaners to come, they didn't. A "do not disturb" sign had been placed on our door. I couldn't fathom why he would do this to me. Couldn't comprehend why anyone would want to cause so much annoyance. I fluctuated through every emotion that day – self-pity, anger, hurt, hatred, frustration, embarrassment, even sadness. I re-played our conversation over breakfast and the evening before. Had something happened that I was unaware of?

Everything had seemed fine. We were laughing and kissing and looking forward to our last day. I sat on the balcony chair, my back to the sun, smelling the jasmine he had bought me. I cried. On that sun drenched honeymoon suite balcony, on the last day of our honeymoon I had nowhere to hide from the rays of the sun. No water, no sun cream. Only my camera and my bunch of jasmine. I turned my body sporadically on the wrought iron balcony chair like I was cooking myself up on a barbeque. Every now and then I looked over the side of the balcony to see if anyone was down below. My pale skin burning. Tingling and stinging. Blistering and sweating. Lips parched and cracked. I called out for someone, anyone but no one seemed to hear.

When the heat and sun was so bad that I thought I might die I rearranged the two heavy chairs and the little round table sometimes lying myself on the boiling tiled floor in their shadow. Eight hours later I was rescued when a lone gardener began to spray the plants. I heard the hose and cried down with a parched voice. The gardener looked up perplexed and was going to ignore me until I pointed and raved like a mad woman. Summoning up strength, fighting back tears. I fainted when they let themselves in, they called a doctor. I drank copious amounts of water and they gave me after-sun cream from the hotel shop. My shins were blistered, my shoulders and back raw. My whole body was an angry red sea of burning, scorched, agonized skin.

He didn't apologize. It had been a misunderstanding. He thought I was behind him. He didn't remember locking the balcony door – sure why would he do that? What type of a person did I think he was? He thought I'd changed my mind about going when I hadn't followed him, and he didn't want to waste the money spent on the excursion. No. He didn't put the "do not disturb" sign on the door, it must have been there from the day before. The hotel staff fussed over him, his concern for me was so great. He called me a "silly sausage" and shook his head in anguish. Wiped away a tear that didn't shimmer. I believed I saw him smirking that night when my teeth were chattering even though heat seared through every fiber of my being. The hotel staff brought him whisky to ease his anxiety, this doting new husband with his wide smile and friendly, good natured banter and craic. He drank the whisky on the balcony as he looked up at the stars and recounted "the most wonderful day of the entire two weeks".

I sipped water between bouts of vomiting and fell asleep with wet towels lying on my burning body.

"Christ but you know how to spoil someone's honeymoon. I can't believe I've married a drama queen. I hope this isn't a sign that there's more of this shit to come." Back then, I hoped that too.

It's funny how our minds play tricks on us. How we can be convinced that something did or didn't happen. How we can rewrite the facts in our mind and create a different story to make our lives easier. More bearable. It takes skill to turn your life's narrative upside down and inside out. I did it. I know I'm not the only one. I've seen it in the eyes of women as they sip their wine, their eyes flicking to their drunk husbands to gauge his mood. I've sensed them smoothing down their skirts and shifting in their seats because they know they've said something wrong or out of line.

Yet they smile. And cajole. And rub his arm to try and smooth things over. They pander to get things on an even keel again. To end the night without being slapped or punched or ridiculed. At the nod of the security guard, I lifted my shopping basket.

"Make sure to use the sanitizer, love."

"No problem at all." The evocative scent of jasmine evaporated as I pumped sanitized on to my palms and rubbed. I'd already guessed what he might like for dinner tonight. Already knew what treat was in store for me when everyone was asleep. But I'd smile.

Fake words would trip off my tongue eagerly to help speed things up. I'd close my eyes and imagine my toes on warm, enveloping sand.

Gratitude

By Aparna Arvind

The breeze was cold, moist and carried the scent of Petrichor informing the arrival of a heavy downpour! I was eagerly waiting for the drizzle as the earthen essence filled my senses with memories and drifted away with jumpy thoughts! I sat there witnessing the leaves of beautiful Night queen tree drenched in shower, the only tree in my humble garden, thinking about my pending assignment, the last night argument with my parents, along with the appetising smell of the Rasam my mother was preparing for lunch. They say aromas reminisces happenings and flashes off our past. Do they bring back the emotions?! The loud thunder and my father's voice grabbed my attention to the now.

As we watched the rainfall and the Night queen tree, my father said, "After the rains, I am uprooting the tree from this place. Your mother and I have been planning for an extra room so that we could rent it and have an additional income". He looked at me waiting for my denial. A pungent aroma filled the room. I wondered if denial and negativity had a smell, would it be like this? Well, it was the aromatic seasoning for the Rasam that my mother was preparing! How could my father think of such a plan?! He knows that I am fond of the tree right from my childhood.

"Dad, Can't you have the extra room built somewhere else?" I tried!

My mother retorted, "Well, we don't have a bungalow here to look for other places!". She was right. Our house was a quaint little home with the bare minimum amenities and a lovely Night Queen tree which my father had bought and planted when the house was built.

As a little girl I have always wanted to have a house with a beautiful garden and a variety of flowering trees and plants. I would envy the girls of my class who brought a bouquet everyday for Margaret Mam who was the new teacher. The girls would bring Roses, Jasmine, which had a sweet scent and sometimes the Nagalinga flowers which gave away a godly presence. Margaret Mam had an aura of a newly blossomed flower. All the kids of the class adored her for extraordinary teaching skills and pleasant ways. She had the capability to spot the needy, feed them with warmth, confidence and make them feel that they are the best! To me, she was like an angel who helped me break from my shell, evolve and progress. She looked like a Jasmine always with bright and pure intentions. Her thoughts and actions were calm, soothing and comforting just like a bunch of the Lavenders. Sure, I wanted to win her heart, but neither did I have a well manicured garden nor the money to buy the precious flowers.

I was alive in the present when I heard my parents discuss about the Night Queen tree, which was about to be the fallen . A wave of sadness crept through me as the perfumed scent of the Night queen made me travel back into time. It seemed impossible for me to gift my beloved teacher with the different fragrances. I was over-come with unexplainable grief thinking of the same. That night, as I drifted to sleep, a divine fragrance filled my nostrils.

Pleasantly surprised, I woke up to find the Night Queen bloom with her beautiful white petal and orange stalk flowers. The days that followed after were heavenly as the flowerets showered unconditionally. The Night queen was tiny, slender which gave away a sweet fra-grance and bloomed at night as she always waited to be picked and gifted. Margaret Mam, took the flowers in both her hands and laid her pink cheeks on the soft petals. She loved them to moon and back. I gifted her with the floral treat every single day! Struck by my father's words, I brought myself back to what he was talk-ing.

He said, "It is just a tree, they are just flowers! Once we are done with all the work, we shall plant a couple of more flowering trees. Don't you worry my little girl!" he patted on my shoulders.

How would I explain to him the gratitude I have for the Night Queen. The next day, arrangements were made by my father for the uprooting of the Night Queen.

I sat there watching the withered Night queen on the ground cursing myself of my incapability to take action. The tree looked dull as if it had already lost its life. The gardeners started to dig the ground and find its roots so that they could completely remove it. The harder they dug, the deeper were its roots, the roots of the tree that gave me hope, love and warmth. My mother and father stood there watching me undergo the agony yet not able to do anything as the work was in progress. It was six in the evening and still they were not able to finish the job.

The gardeners finally declared, "Sir, this tree is too strong to give up. If we dig further, it will cause cracks in your compound wall. You might have to build it again" he said. Those were the tense moments of my life. I looked at the night sky with the stars twinkling down at me with some certainty. Now, I was longing for a shooting star to grant my wishes. They were discussing on the same point. My mother was urging the workers to find an alternative solution. I was still looking at them praying for a miracle! My father's eyes met mine for a second.

He suddenly declared, "No, let's stop with this and see what we can do about it. I will bring the mason tomorrow to discuss about the same".

Tears rolled down my eyes filled with happiness and peace. That night, I pondered at the night sky which shone with moonlight and the gentle breeze brushed my face. The sweet scent of gratitude swept through me for yet another time.

The Empty Space

By Varsha Murthy

T he old man stood looking at his shelving unit.

It was perfect, every bottle laid out perfectly, evenly spaced, completely devoid of dust. He didn't demand much from his maid, preferring to let her do her own thing, slack off occasionally even, but this? This he required of her. And by now she knew that even if she didn't dust his furniture every day, or put his clothes in the closet immediately after they were done drying, if she just came and dusted off the contents of this room every day, she would still have a job.

He wondered sometimes what his reputation was, what she said about her employer to her friends and family. More likely than not, she'd probably shrug her shoulders, call him eccentric and move on from the topic. It was a job after all and no one liked to dwell on these things longer than necessary. Especially if they were making your life easier in some way.

Eccentricity was something you could claim after your bank account crossed a certain limit, going from dangerous to weird to eccentric. Maybe a quirky thrown in there somewhere. Good looks and money bought you that and he'd never had to worry about the former. And yeah, eccentric billionaire had a nice ring to it.

These were his treasures, these bottles of perfumes he kept carefully in a separate room just off his bedroom. In truth, it had been a walk-in closet where his clothes were supposed to go, about the size of his first apartment all those years ago. His clothes could all be stuffed into the cupboard in the corner near his bed, being not very many and not very dear, but not these. Not his treasures.

He started at the corner of the room, near his very first one. He still remembered the day he got it.

He had finished his first big con, easily taking everything the man had with an easy smile and a little, self-deprecating shrug of his shoulders as he said something like, "Ah well guess I got lucky this time, hmm?" Beginner's luck when he was neither a beginner, nor lucky.

He'd been walking down the street, wondering what to do with his first big score when he'd seen it. Or, smelt it rather. The open doors of the perfumery let out a mix of floral and fruity smells and he just couldn't walk past it all. So, he'd gone in.

The smell inside was stronger and the shop was cool and dark inside. It was the kind of store where not many people could go so the salesclerks were all milling around, talking amongst themselves. When he entered, they stopped, turned and looked at him and he could see them looking him up and down, taking him in, deciding he wasn't the kind of person who belonged in their store.

He remembered being a little intimidated at first but, like always, he never let it show. The first rule of lying was to look like you're not. Don't look as if you might be hiding something and people won't think you are.

He just walked right up to the counter and asked to be shown their best. They'd looked at each other, wondering if they should serve him, if he'd be able to buy what they had, but ultimately shrugged and decided to do it. What's the worst that could happen, right? There weren't even any other customers in the store that might be scandalized at the kind of riffraff they let in.

So, he stood there smelling all these samples, as the clerks asked him if there was a special lady he was buying for, if she had any preferences. He'd said sure, let's go with that, no she didn't have any.

He'd come away that day with a little round glass bottle, one of those pumps on it that you'd press to spray it, filled with an orangey scent with floral notes.

He could have conned it off them. He knew even then that he could have conned it off them. And yet, he found himself walking up to the counter, handing over the exact price. When he walked out, the clerks had all stopped judging him from afar and waved goodbye to him as if they were all old friends.

He stood now looking at that very same bottle. Its contents had spoiled over the years and he couldn't use it but no matter. He still remembered exactly what it smelt like, how the pump felt under his fingers as he pressed it. He carefully moved it an inch to the left.

He wasn't quite sure when perfumes had become his trophies or why he acquired them the way he had. He could get people to give them to him, con them right out of their hands but... not these. These, he preferred to get the good, old-fashioned, honest way. Even if the money itself may not have been acquired entirely honestly.

Carefully he shifted each bottle, each one bringing back memories of each of his escapades. The pink with the gold lid he'd got the first time he'd done something big enough to have to escape.

Rose still always reminded him of that. The violet glass one that he'd got at the airport that first time he'd left someone he'd gotten too close to. Violet wasn't something you'd associate with the mango-pineapple scent inside so he'd bought that one. The clear glass that he got outside the museum the first time he'd been hired as a distraction during a heist because he had a reputation now. Even now, it made him smile proudly. And just because it was illegal doesn't mean he couldn't look at his work with pride, right?

People over the years had seen his collection. And there was nothing out of the ordinary about a perfume collection. People collected lots of things, from books to stamps, coins. Toys, even. The fact that he collected perfumes wasn't the issue. The issue was that, when people knew you liked something, they tended to give it to. Birthdays, holidays, he'd received quite a few fragrances in his time. And it was sweet but- that's not what his collection was for. That's not why he bought them. So, receiving one was a tiresome cycle of "Gee thanks" and then finding someone who might want it while convincing the person who had given it that of course he had it, he wore it all the time and the only reason he wasn't wearing it right now was just that certain moods called for certain things, you know how it is. So, while the thought is what counts, he'd much prefer something else. He'd be damned if he let one that he hadn't bought himself, that didn't mean anything, sit here among the rest.

Among them all was a cheap stick of deodorant, seemingly out of place-and not even the kind that actually smells good-and here he stopped, taking it in his hands and rubbing the rounded plastic top. He wished he didn't have it there but...

As he'd been leaving his prison cell he'd almost, almost walked out without it. He'd gotten right up to the gate before he turned back and quickly stuffed it into his pocket. Then, he'd almost thrown it away but he'd dived for the bin at the last second, pulling it out and putting it here (after washing it, of course). Not willing to part with it but not wanting to see it either so it sat in a corner far away from the rest of them.

The deodorant had been bought at the prison store out of pure necessity (really, it was required) that one time he had let his guard down. They'd caught him and convicted him and he'd ended up in jail and he'd known it was a mistake while it was happening but…

He'd stayed anyway. He'd stayed and he'd waited and he'd been there just long enough to get caught. There was a reason that Conning 101's first rule was to never let anyone get close to you.

People were weaknesses and letting them in set you up for mistakes. The second rule was to run as soon as the job was done. He'd broken one and then the other and he had one cheap, smelly deodorant to show for it.

If things went right this time, that would be the only one of those on his shelves. He was…old now. Yes, that made things easier for him in some ways because if something went missing, you wouldn't suspect the sweet old man who had just retired and was doing something fun, for himself for a change, that his kids had booked this for him, to get him out of the house after his wife…

No, you'd probably apologize TO him say you're sorry this had happened, apologize for the inconvenience and of course he could go, would he like you to call him a cab?

But at his age…if things went wrong, he'd likely be spending the last of his years behind bars. All he'd have to look at and smell was another of these, one more cheap, chemical smelling stick of deodorant.

It wasn't that he needed the money. He was rich and he didn't have anyone to leave it to (see Conning Rule No. 1). But he'd never been able to say no when old friends came knocking and he'd definitely never been able to say no to...

He'd been responsible for Deodorant No. 1, anyway. What difference would a second one make?

Never mind. This was it. He was done with his prep after carefully moving each bottle a little to the left so they'd all be equidistant and perfect once again.

The old man stood looking at his shelving unit. It was perfect, every bottle laid out perfectly, evenly spaced, completely devoid of dust. There was a new, empty space at the end now. The only thing to be seen was whether it would be filled by a stick of deodorant or a nice perfume in a glass bottle.

Daphne

By Fía Ruve

Many lovers have existed before in my life, yet no one compares to Daphne. There was not a doubt in my mind that Daphne was not only the one that I wanted, but also the one that I wished to be too. She was the most incredible being my eyes had ever laid sight on. She had something special—that something that is impossible to figure out. Her silhouette, her color, and her odor exceeded in every way her competitors for my attention, and even myself. She had it all, and perhaps even too much.

After a gray cold day of working a miserably paying job, I had made my way to go buy my dinner at the supermarket. Walking through the extended hallways searching for anything to exterminate this unstoppable appetite, my eyes caught of something that would finally satisfy me - a glimpse of her. It was the first time that she had been there, or perhaps she was there previously, yet she had never looked that appealing to the eye. Not only was she delightful, but her aroma was so potent that it invaded the whole room. The store was more crowded that afternoon, than any other day before, yet she was so radiant and colorful that it was impossible for me to ignore it. I approached a person from the staff, who told me her name was Daphne.

"Daphne," "Daphne"... what a delightful name for a delightful being! My eyes were insistent on admiring her beauty, until they were forced abruptly to stop by another customer passing by. Even with this desire to stay, to appreciate her beauty, and to approach her, I continued shopping for my groceries and left the place soon after. On the way back home, the sky was turning gray as the night loomed from the horizon. My steps got faster trying to avoid the unavoidable truth that it was going to rain very soon. As the clouds moved closer, my skin could feel the cold even with all the layers of clothing as if spikes of ice were penetrating the fabric, but that didn't bother me because all that was in my mind was Daphne. Her image was imprinted in my memory and refused to be erased. While being already so far away from her, her reminiscence was so attached to me that I could still sense her odor in the air as the wind blew.

After having eaten the meal from the supermarket, I went to bed in order to get some rest for the new day of work that was going to begin in a few hours. However, this was not an easy task to achieve. Everytime my eyes closed, a vibrant picture of Daphne would appear in front of them instead of the usual darkness in my head combined with the black night. Even at times where my body rested, she would emerge in my usual solitary dreams, and her strong fragrance was still lingering so vividly that it didn't feel like a recollection anymore. The enchantment of her vision and her odor put me to sleep with the passing of the minutes, and before knowing it, the next morning had arrived. That day, before going to work, I walked back to the supermarket to see Daphne.

I moved around the store looking for her, until she peaked out from afar. The rays of sun were illuminating her through the window displaying her beauty. She was more exquisite than the prior day. Closing my eyes, her perfume invaded my lungs, and it became clear then that she needed to go with me. While getting closer to her, I became aware of something that had not been apparent to me the first time seeing her: there were more of them —they were "Daphnes" —all of them equally alluring. My fingers moved feeling their outline, and appreciating once more their marvellous tones and fragrance. Their petals were incredibly delicate and soft, yet they were so strong and stable. Other types of flowers surrounded the Daphnes, yet they had nothing special. Next to the Daphnes, it was difficult to even take notice of the others. These were the most ravishing flowers that I had encountered. Without a lot of reflection, it was clear that they were coming with me to the home.

After paying for them, I grabbed them with both arms and embraced them tenderly while walking my way back. And as they laid in my arms, the closeness of the Daphnes to my nose would intoxicate me into a feeling of euphoria that had been unknown to me prior. My senses would become much more receptive and with their odor my perceptions would suddenly become more colorful and beautiful. I fell in love for the first time. I laid the pots next to the window and next to my bed, and sat in front of them to admire them.

Without realizing it, it had gotten too late to attend my work, but that was very far from my concerns. My eyes could not stop observing and my mind could not stop trying to understand my deep appeal for Daphne. There was something different in her - something I had never identified before The next couple of days were filled with trips to obtain more Daphnes, and in each one, my desire to gather more increased. My room had gotten overflown by flowers, but with every one of them, their beauty augmented. In my sleep, visions of their pink color and their fragrance would intoxicate my dreams to a point in which my attention was focused on them at every moment of my life, which was stopping me from all the other parts of it. Thus, I needed to find a way for Daphne to be with me at every moment. Her company had become essential in my existence.

With various tools from the kitchen, I started extracting Daphnes' fragrance and pouring it into narrowed containers that I could add to my clothes, shampoo, soaps, creams, and perfumes. Without Daphne, there was nothing in me that was needed. Daphnes gave me all and more. Everywhere, people would ask me what the smell was, and it was always her delightful aroma. Her fragrance was the only redeemable quality about me. Her balm became the only interesting aspect in my life, and I was happy with that because I agreed. It continued this way for various months.

My Daphnes would give me their smell, and I would give them my space and my time. Daphne was my company, my lover. Their marvellous look and alluring odor had become my obsession—Daphnes had everything I wanted, yet suddenly, Daphnes' company was no longer enough for me. Her continuous presence was no longer satisfying my desires. Unexpectedly, in between the perfumes of these beautiful flowers, it all began to make sense in my mind. She had everything I wanted, but more important than that, she had everything I wanted to be.

Daphne was delicate, strong, alluring, beautiful, and

powerful. There was nothing else that I wished more. Their fragrance and appearance was not sufficient for me anymore. My destiny was to be one of and with the Daphnes. I took the liquid that contained its fragrance and poured it all on a small syringe. The barrel got filled slowly with the yellowish liquid which without knowing it, held my biggest wish inside. It looked so fresh, savory, and appealing that my mouth had started watering just from imagining what it contained.

The Daphnes around me seemed to be getting closer as if they were waiting to embrace me as one of their own. They were expelling an aroma different than the usual one, but still as glorious and intoxicating. It seemed as if my transformation had already begun. Soon, I was going to be a Daphne. Forcing the needle punctured my skin, the liquid started entering my veins rapidly. Its passing felt like it was burning as it moved inside my body. My heart rate was rising as it fought against my awaited change. This ache simply seemed adequate for the extreme alteration that my system was experiencing. I clenched my fists and shut my eyes, trying to divert myself from the pain that was invading me, but this agony was filled with euphoria of knowing that I was going to be soon part of the Daphnes.

The visions and aromas of Daphne were becoming more powerful within myself every second. I laid on the floor in order to prepare myself to be around the other Daphnes when I had completely shifted. As I stayed still I began sensing everything that was occurring inside and outside of me. My legs were transforming into a steady stem and my hands were becoming ample leaves. Underneath my feet, I could feel small roots growing long to hold me. Then, tiny pink petals started coming out of my head liberating the same fragrance as the other Daphnes, as well as a style in the middle. Suddenly, I had lost all my vision and my movements, yet I could see myself clearly. I was Daphne.

The gift of aroma

By Swathi H.

She tucked her hair behind her ear. The wind was playing with the jasmine flowers in her hand. How beautiful a day it would have been if she was just a girl of twelve without a care in the world. She knew normal from the people she saw around her— the ones who bought her flowers. They had smiles on their faces and somebody to give flowers to. Occasionally, they would tell her why they needed the flowers. The teenager in the black shirt wanted roses to give his beloved. He picked the red ones carefully, the ones with tender petals and strong stems. A girl with plaited hair thought that the jasmine flowers would look good on her. A middle-aged man bought marigolds for his wife to wake up to. Isn't that what life is all about?

Thinking of someone and going back to them. Going home. Home. Now's not a great time to think of home, she thought. She had to sell the jasmine flowers when they were still fresh. It wasn't Onam season when flowers sold like hot cakes. No, now she had to go to reluctant observers brandishing the flowers. Today was one of the lucky days. The priest of the temple bought a huge strip of her jasmines. She muttered a prayer under her breath and scuttled along. Finally, she could get home before evening.

Few steps further down the road, Manu was coming down from the bustle of a wedding. He couldn't take in the smoke anymore. The room seemed to get smaller with people. Beneath the silk shirt his mother loved, he felt as if he was melting. Beads of sweat came up on his forehead. At least, he could have the feast— the only thing that kept him going. That's when he saw a girl of his age. Her hair was loose around her tanned face. He watched as she walked by with the flowers swaying. She looked right at him as she felt his eyes on her. Manu averted his gaze a second too late. She was walking towards him.

"Do you want the jasmines?" she asked, smiling.

"Not really," he said. Her face dropped but she gave him a faint smile. She was turning away when he said, "On second thoughts, I'll take them. How much do they cost?"

She picked the jasmines stitched together and pointed to an arm's length of jasmines and said, "10 rupees".

There couldn't possibly be over three of them left, he noticed. That would make 30 rupees. In his pocket, there were three ten-rupee notes; money he had been saving to buy a Kinder Joy. It was one of those things you could never expect your middle-class parents to get. He had only had it once, and his mouth watered in remembrance. Yet something in him moved when he saw the girl. She seemed like she had been out in the sun for long now, dust caked on her face. Needless to say, the sun was merciless.

"I'll take the lot." He said. He gave her the money and she gave him the last batch of flowers. He didn't know what he would do with three strips of jasmine. One for his mother and one for his little sister.

"Could you cut this for me?" He asked. She rummaged through her sling bag and took the scissors. She cut the thread quite a few times before it tore apart. She gave him the piece but he shook his head.

"Aren't you going to take this? You already paid me for it." she pointed out.

"I know. I only need two. You can keep it with you. Consider it a present. The gift of aroma." He gave her the flower and checked his watch. They would serve lunch soon. He waved at her and climbed the stairs. She watched him as he disappeared. Someone had given her a present. The gift of aroma as he called it. She inhaled the sweet fragrance of the jasmine. Something she hadn't paid attention to in a long, long time. Something so familiar yet enchanting. She did not have anything left to do. She could head home early, picking up food for her mother on the way. Yet she found herself thinking of selling the jasmine for the extra money. It was quickly followed by another thought. What would he think? She brushed it off. He would forget all about this in no time. Who remembers the girl selling flowers they met for a minute? Hardly anyone. Under the shade of a banyan tree, she ate her packed lunch. Porridge and a pickle. She walked around with that last strip of jasmine, searching for an owner. The owner ended up being the old man in a tea stall near the temple. When he smiled, she could see all his uneven teeth clearly. Through the side of her eyes, she thought she saw the boy. She dared not to look in that direction. With her head down, she walked in the opposite direction, slowly picking up her pace. She relaxed as the heaviness in her chest died down. Her mother was fast asleep when she walked in. She softly joined her in bed with her eyes wide open. It could have been hours or just a few minutes. It felt like one big moment. Soon her mother stirred in her sleep and woke up. "When did you come in?" She asked. "Not too long ago." She heard herself say. "Happy birthday jaan" her mother said. She rarely called her jaan. "Amma I got a gift today." "Really? From the girls down the street?" She asked. She shook her head, sobbing like the baby her mother knew when she was five. In the warm circle of her mother's arms, she was rocked to sleep. They call the jasmine the Queen of the night for no reason. It wafted the fragrance of the gods. From the backyard, the flowers released its earthy scent. This time she didn't fight it. She inhaled it all in. The flowers lulled her into sleep.

Perfectionist's Poison

By Chrissy Kett

My heart thuds as panic clutches my chest. I don't want to watch this. But I must. I have no choice but to sit here and witness a ceremony so repulsive that my stomach churns before it's even begun. "Megan Adeomi."

The name is announced, and I hear the inevitable sobbing. I follow the sound, looking to the rows behind me. There. I spot her among the hundreds of other students, as she stands and shuffles to the end of her row. She starts the long walk to the stage, as we try to ignore the thud of her footsteps, and the gulping sound as she chokes on her tears. I drop my gaze before she passes me. Terrified to gaze at the pain lurking in her eyes.

Instead, like a coward, I look at everything else. Anything else. My eyes sweep around the assembly hall: black walls, white chairs, and black marble floor of the stage, all swirl amid rows of black and white uniforms. Students appear as waves in a sea of perverse perfectionism. Not one colour besmirches the canvas where students are duplicated with robotic accuracy. All the same. All judged by the same criteria. All punished by the exams written by the same men who do not know us, and never will.

The exams where just one point, one tick-box, makes the difference between a pass and a... My eyes dart to the front as Megan reaches the stage. An unnatural silence suffocates the hall. I can no longer keep my eyes distracted. They're pulled towards her face like metal to a magnet. The fear in her eyes freezes my blood. I know what happens next. I know what's coming. Dread pumps through me like adrenaline. Please let it be quick. Please just let it be over. But it will never be over. This is just the beginning. The single moment that marks the rest of her life. She'll never recover. Once it's done, her life can never, and will never be the same.

"Students, your attention please," Mrs Chandra announces. She's trying to be strong. Trying to be brave, but her cracking voice betrays her. "You are aware that since the syllabus has changed, the marking criteria has become stricter still. Megan, it is with deep regret that I have to inform you that you've failed."

"It was just one question," Megan sobs. "I got everything else right. I'm sure I did. Didn't I?"

"It's true. You would have received a Distinction in total marks, but you know that in accordance to the new syllabus, I can't pass you unless you can fully answer every criteria question."

"Please don't do it," Megan begs. "Ask me again. Ask me now. I know I can do it."

"It's too late Megan. You've already failed," Mrs Chandra says. "My hands are tied. We have no jurisdiction over the curriculum."

It was all she could do to prevent the algorithms, and she nearly lost her job for it. Teachers no longer have the power to protect their students; it's been over a decade since we had any allies who could actually help us.

"I really am very sorry Megan," Mrs Chandra says, as I see her heart breaking. Then she sets her face as though it were a stone statue.

The government officers walk onto stage, wearing their suits of indifference. Megan screams. She starts to lash out as hands grip her. An officer tries to usher Mrs Chandra off the stage, but she will not be moved. She holds eye contact with Megan, as the young student is forced into the procedure chair and strapped into place.

Is that why teachers are still here? Why they endure it all? Just so we're not alone as we suffer through endless tests, hoops and hurdles in this obstacle course of insanity? Just so they can continue to help us despite minimal resources and depleting energy reserves?

Megan sits in the chair: restraints grip her legs, arms and head. She continues to struggle, but she can't free herself. A large glass cube is lowered from the fly tower of the stage, and her screams fade into silence as the cube encases her. It could be an opaque cube. It could be done in a separate room all together. But then we couldn't watch. Then we couldn't learn from this spectacle of failure. Glass, it is then. Perfectly transparent to witness her perfect failure. One question wrong. That's all there is to it. Fail.

A doctor enters the glass cube through a sliding door. She's completely covered in a hazmat suit. Protected from what's to come. Megan opens her mouth. She screams. But we hear nothing through the glass. I think the silence is even worse. My hearing dulled, my vision zooms in for further clarity, forever engraining her contorted face in my mind. This is it. The doctor walks towards her, holding the metal suitcase. Soon. A camera now starts to film the process, and projects the footage onto the back wall of the stage, as if her misery were no more than entertainment. The entire school watches as the suitcase is opened, and the camera zooms in. A tiny glass vial.

The doctor picks it up with the utmost care, and walks towards Megan. She unscrews the lid, and prepares the pipette. There it is. The odious perfume. The fragrance of failure. She administers a single drop to Megan's neck, two further drops to each wrist, and then with gloved hands carefully rubs the fragrance into the innocent skin. That's it. It's done. She's marked for life. Branded with a scent that will be forever recognised. A stench that will follow her everywhere she goes and corrupt every future endeavour. The reek of failure. It will never come off, no matter how much she scrubs at her skin. I've seen others try. I've seen their scratched, broken, and bleeding skin betraying their desperation to remove the stink that follows them down the corridor. The stench that makes everyone avoid them as if they were an animal. Dehumanising them with every single step. You might imagine this fragrance to be potent, comparable perhaps to decaying fish, rotten eggs, or even faeces. But it's not. It's subtle.

At first whiff, you might not even notice it, but once you've learnt it, it's instantly recognisable. It's a fragrance to evoke dark fears and sinister memories, making you gag with nausea, though you can't explain why. Megan's stopped screaming. The glass cube still swallows all sound, but now she just stares ahead with dead, unseeing eyes. A gaze so lifeless it makes me wish she was still screaming.

The doctor returns the glass vial to the suitcase, placing it carefully in the padded compartment. Then she stands perfectly still, as jets of air are fired into the cube. Decontaminating a process so vile, no amount of sterile air could ever clean it. The cube is lifted back into the fly tower, and the doctor removes her mask. There are tears in her eyes as she glares at the government officers. She's following orders too.

"There. That wasn't so bad was it?" one of the suits announces to the assembly hall. "You'll think twice now, won't you Megan, before you revise for your next test. You may return to your seat."

Mrs Chandra and the doctor stare at him with such fire in their eyes I almost expect him to melt under their gaze, but for that he'd need some modicum of self-awareness, and integrity.

Megan makes her way down the steps, her hands shaking as she grips the rail, and starts the long walk back to her row. I see the heads flinching away as she passes. I'm determined to meet her gaze, but as soon as she draws near, the stench makes me gag, and I have to cover my face so I don't vomit. I steal a glance over my shoulder. She sits down next to former friends who now squirm away from her.

"We must continue," the suit demands our attention again. "Mrs Chandra, please go on with the next name."

Again, I see Mrs Chandra force all emotion out of her eyes as she prepares to announce the next failure. "Sarah Williams."

Me? No it can't be. I revised for hours for the test. I studied every question. I did everything perfectly. I'm sure I did. This can't be true. This can't be happening. I sit rooted to the spot. I can't move. I won't move. I won't allow them to do that to me. I won't let them brand me with that poison for the rest of my life.

"Miss Williams, you are holding up the proceedings," the suit complains. "We must run to schedule."

"But it isn't true. I'm not a failure," I find my voice.

"You are. And it is my duty to make sure that you are punished to avoid future failures."

"How can we avoid future failures when you're setting us up to fail?"

"I will not have this insolence. If you look at the statistics you can see that..."

"But we're not statistics. We're not numbers. We're people. We're individuals. Why are you obsessed with measuring our scores on a curriculum that is as corrupt as it is outdated?"

"Enough," he shouts. "This is the way it is. This is what education means. You must meet criteria. And if you want to pass you must answer every single criteria question correctly. You did not, and therefore you are a failure and must face those consequences. Accept your fate gracefully, or my officers will have no choice but to manhandle you."

"I do not accept that I am a failure, and I will never accept it."

"Then you leave me no choice." Fear surges through me as officers start marching towards me. I try to run. I try to escape, but I can't claw my way free from their outstretched hands... I gasp as they grip my shoulder.

"Oh sorry darling, didn't mean to make you jump." I take a breath, and come back to my surroundings.

"That's ok, Mum. Just revising."

"Dinner's ready," she says as she closes the textbook in front of me.

"Come on, that's enough now. Try not to worry about

this exam tomorrow. What's the worst that could happen?"

I smile. She seriously underestimates my imagination.

A stinky murder case

By Shilpa Keshav

"**T**he Stinky murder case keeps getting mysterious day after day. What is the department doing about this?" A reporter asked the Police Commissioner.

"We are getting into the depth of the matter, which we can't disclose right now. Please have some patience," the Commissioner replied and scurried away.

"The media is trailing us like a pack of hyenas. We need to do something about this. Summon Inspector Briana from the Special Task Force immediately," Commissioner Saxena commanded.

Inspector Briana Jacob was a known name in the city. A sincere and headstrong woman, she was an officer of indomitable spirit. Dauntless and tenacious, Briana possessed an astute problem-solving skill and a brilliant observant mind, that recorded even minute details that others may have overlooked. This made her the obvious choice as an investigation officer for this particular case.

"Briana, I hope you have been following the serial murder case," Saxena said.

"Yes sir, it's all over the television," Briana replied.

"I want you to head this case, Briana. And I expect immediate results as always."

Constable Shankar got the case file for her.

"Madam, I'm so glad to be working with you again. I get to learn so much," Shankar said.

"Thanks, Shankar. This case has been floating around the media a lot."

"Yes madam. They have named it "The Stinky Murder" because all the dead bodies have been discovered in a dump yard. It seems the killer loves garbage!" Shankar shook his head cursing the killer.

"Let's get to the beginning, Shankar. There have been five murders till now- four being women, and one man.

All the bodies were recovered from Bandra dump yard and were covered with garbage. The modus operandi is the same. The victims were gagged with a cloth and their hands were tied from behind before the murder. Their bodies were doused with petrol, but there were no signs of burning. They were stabbed to death," Briana paused.

"Did you find any common thread between the victims?"

"None, madam," Shankar replied. The victims were unknown to each other according to family members. No personal enmity too."

"Hmm... all of them were killed at night. The first victim was a call centre employee, the second, a college girl returning back home after a party, the third victim was a man working in an IT firm, the fourth woman was a high-end call girl and the last one was a sales girl in a perfume shop. Did you notice that though each one of them worked in different suburbs of Mumbai, they were murdered in Bandra?" Briana said pointing at the city map. "Their offices were mostly between Malad, Andheri and

Dadar."

"Does that mean the killer lives in Bandra?" Shankar asked.

"Can't say anything, Shankar. I would like to meet the people who were with the victims before murder," Briana said.

***

Briana met Pallavi, who was with the first victim, Rhea, an hour before she was murdered.

"We work at the call centre. That night, unfortunately our pick-up vehicle had broken down and we went back home on our own," Pallavi said. "Both Rhea and I walked to the bus stop. She was tired, so she didn't wait for the bus. She went home in a taxi, while I waited for a bus."

"But Rhea never reached home, she was killed before that," Briana said. "Rhea called you later, right?"

"Yes, she was scared. She said the driver started behaving weirdly. He was trembling," Pallavi replied.

"Trembling?" Briana was perplexed.

"Even I was surprised. I asked her about it, but the line got disconnected. I tried calling again, but her cell was switched off."

Briana spoke with other people too, who were last seen with the victims. And all of them had mentioned one common factor- a taxi!

**

Back in the office, Briana was lost in a myriad of thoughts. All clues pointed towards a taxi. Was its driver the killer? There was no CCTV near the dump yard. But why that place? Just then, her colleague, Meera came.

"Briana, do you have a painkiller? My head is aching."

"Yes dear, I always keep one in my bag," Briana handed

her the medicine.

"We ladies usually keep makeup items in our bag. Glad to know you are different," Meera thanked Briana and left.

Like lightening, a thought struck Briana, and she rushed to the police evidence room where the belongings of the victims were kept. After thoroughly checking, she found one item common in all the ladies' bags- a perfume bottle! However, they were of different brands. She took them to the forensic laboratory.

"We need to do Chemical Trace Analysis to find out the key ingredients in them, Briana," the forensic doctor said.

"Give me a couple of days."

***

Two days later, Briana was at the laboratory.

"Though the perfume brands are different, they have a common ingredient- Coumarin," the doctor said.

"Could you please explain in detail, doctor?" Briana asked.

"Coumarin is an aromatic chemical compound commonly found in perfumes. It has a mild Vanilla fragrance. All the victims probably were smelling alike," the doctor said.

"Do you think the killer was repulsive to this fragrance? Or perhaps he was allergic to Coumarin?"

"Could be. Coumarin as such is harmless, but some people suffer from fragrance allergy. Such people are called hyperosmic, which is a medical condition wherein a person is hypersensitive to a particular smell."

"And what complications are seen in such patients, doctor?"

"When such people come in contact with that smell, it may trigger migraine, or vomiting, or in rare cases, cause extreme anxiety or depression, driving them violent and insane. This may arise due to genetic or neurological disorder; the causes are many."

Briana tried to join the dots. A fragrance was common in all the victims. The dead women's perfumes and the man's deodorant contained Coumarin, that probably drove the taxi driver insane. Hence, he was trembling anxiously, as mentioned by Rhea. He doused them with petrol and dumped them amidst trash, perhaps as a distressed reaction to the extreme repulsion towards the fragrance.

"Shankar, I need to view the CCTV footages of locations and streets near Bandra dump yard on all nights the murders took place- near traffic signal or ATM or restaurants. I need to track that taxi number," Briana said.

Soon, she had the footages.

"These locations are close to the dump yard, and each footage has a common taxi, madam. After this, the taxi takes an exit towards the dump yard," Shankar pointed out.

"Excellent job, Shankar," Briana said. She noted down the taxi number, as Shankar beamed proudly.

"I need another help, Shankar," Briana said.

"You just order madam."

"I need someone, preferably a woman, who can board this taxi and help us nab the criminal," Briana said.

Shankar thought for a while and said, "Consider it done, madam. My wife, Durga would be the best choice."

"Are you sure? It's a bit risky job."

"Leave that to me, madam."

At home, munching food, Shankar told his wife,

"There is an important mission at work, and we need a brave woman to volunteer."

***

"What mission?" Durga inquired curiously.

"Oh, it's simple. But the reward and recognition are mind blowing. All she needs to do is board a taxi and get down after a while."

"That's all?"

Shankar nodded.

"*Aho*, what about me?" Durga put an extra paratha in his plate.

"You?" Shankar pretended to think.

"Why not? Am I not brave? Recommend my name to your madam, or else I will go to my aai's house," she threatened. "Our neighbours will be so jealous seeing me in newspapers," she giggled.

"Hope they don't see you in the obituary page," Shankar murmured.

"What?" she thundered pointing the rolling pin towards him.

"I... I said I shall speak to madam tomorrow itself," Shankar quietly ate his food.

***

On the D-day, Durga was sent to a salon for some grooming. A new saree with proper makeup and hairstyle boosted her confidence and happiness.

"My stingy husband has never bought an expensive saree till now," she admonished Shankar. "God bless Briana madam, and may she pass some good sense to this fellow!"

***

The taxi driver, Tony was tracked. That night, Briana,

Shankar and Durga met at Dadar taxi stand. Briana handed over a silver purse to Durga with a small bottle of perfume.

"Remember to spray this amply on yourself when you are inside the taxi," Briana said.

Durga was elated. "This looks expensive!" Her eyes shone. "Can I keep this once my job is done?"

"Take it along as a parting gift," Shankar sighed.

"This man never made sense to me. Anyway, I'm off." Durga ambled towards the taxi stand. She read the taxi number and as instructed, approached it. "Bhaiyya, take me to Bandra station, please."

Tony nodded. Once seated inside, Durga took out a hand mirror and admired her new look. Never had she looked this pretty. She praised Briana for her kindness. For such a trivial mission, she got a free salon visit as well as a branded purse and perfume. How jealous her neighbors would be! Just then, her phone rang. It was her neighbor, Meena.

"Hello, Meena," Durga whispered. "Listen, I can't talk to you right now. I'm on a secret mission. What? No, no, I cannot disclose anything right now..."

The taxi halted at once. "Get down," Tony hissed.

"What? But this is not Bandra station," Durga looked around.

"I said get out," he barked angrily.

Suddenly, Durga remembered that she had to spray the perfume before leaving. She took out the bottle and sprayed generously all over her.

Tony got restless. His body began to shiver, much to Durga's astonishment. His face distorted and mouth twitched. Sneezing and coughing profusely, he rushed out and started throwing up.

"Bhaiyya, are you fine?" Durga asked confused.

Tony threw a nasty stare with his bloodshot eyes that startled Durga. As she tried to run, he caught her and pushed her inside the taxi. He took a bottle that contained petrol and sprinkled everywhere. He tied her hands with a rope and gagged her mouth with his muffler as she gaped at him in terror. He flicked her mobile off the speeding vehicle. Briana traced Durga's mobile location and reached the spot where it was thrown. It lay on the deserted road, broken.

"Durga! Where could she be? We... we have lost track of her," Shankar stuttered.

"Don't worry, Shankar. I have a backup ready. Her purse is fitted with a GPS location tracker." Briana was always a step ahead of the rest, and that's what made her special.

***

Tony halted his taxi near the dump yard. He dragged Durga out by pulling her hair mercilessly. He drew a dagger from the corner of his seat. His eyes were still blood red and hands shaky. Murmuring like a deranged psycho, his twisted lips smiled scornfully. As he raised his dagger, a gunshot reverberated in the darkness. A loud scream followed. Tony lay dead in a pool of blood. Durga opened her eyes.

"Are you fine?" Shankar asked.

"I was almost killed and you are asking me this question?"

"You did a great job, Durga. We are proud of you," Briana patted her back.

"Was capturing this psycho the mission that you spoke about?" Durga threw an incredulous stare at

Shankar. "And knowingly you sent me for this?"

Shankar scratched his head searching for an answer.

"Don't bother to reply. Just come home, you $@#& %..."

"Madam, please post me somewhere else for another mission. I don't want to go home," Shankar cupped his ears and pleaded.

***

"STINKY MURDER CASE SOLVED. PSYCHO SERIAL KILLER DIES IN ENCOUNTER. INSPECTOR BRIANA DISPLAYS HER METTLE YET AGAIN!"

The newspapers proudly flashed the officer's valorous accomplishment, as Briana set out on her next mission.

The Fragrance of Amma's Sarees

By Lavanya Girish

"Creak, Creak" came the sound!

"What is that noise? Someone's coming to this room", whispered the inmates of the room.

To be more precise they were the sole occupants of the old cupboard in the abandoned room for time immemorial. A whole lot of sarees in different colors, different hues and varied textures. All of them nurtured their own specific stories. Some of them were procured for their scent and their fragrance. Yes, although it was an indeed a strange way to purchase a Saree, yet the fresh odor of each saree appealed to the beautiful buyer who ultimately conquered them and made them her own.

"Hush, sisters", said the Queen Bee of them all, the Red Kanchivaram pattu saree. Dominant she was, Oh yes! After all she was MY AMMA's bridal saree that formed part of her wedding trousseau.

"But Akka, why will anyone come here? Don't they abhor us? We are castaways", lamented the Bangladeshi Dhaakai, which Amma had lovingly bought on one of her trips to Chittagong.

The noise echoed in the corridor and inched closer and closer. The sarees were all perplexed. They were hundreds of them, lying stoic waiting to feel wanted again. They belonged to different backgrounds and comprised varied tapestry and gossamer. They all had a different story to tell. Amma was an amalgamation of cultures. Brought up in the south, but had slowly made her way into several hearts in the East, imbibing the diversity as time went by.

The Red and Ivory hued Aar Paar Saree reminisced olden days.

"You know sisters? I was specially chosen for the Dhunuchi dance. Though not an ardent fan of dancing, Amma never hesitated to take part in the Sindoor Khela. It was a moment when she was oblivious to everything around her and she found herself swaying to the beats of the Dhak during Durga Pooja. I was her constant companion wrapped up around her body but closest to her soul. Oh, I still remember, she used to smell me while folding me after my use. I was never washed, cherished as a memento always, desired for the fragrance that I obtained after each usage."

The Blue colored Taant saree whispered – "I was meant for serene moments. Amma draped me when she enjoyed those moments of solitude. It was bestowed once in a blue moon and she would invariably make the best out of such moments. She would put on a big Bindi, apply Alta and would read a book by the quaint balcony space, humming to herself "Jodi tor daak shune keo naa aashe, tobe akela cholo re", Tagore's famous song.

The Sambhalpuri saree went next. "I was no less her favorite. Bought on one of her trips to Puri, she used to revel in the joy of simply caressing my maroon body albeit embellished golden borders. Big jhumkas and anklets used to accessorize the look making her emulate 'Royalty and Grandeur'. The Bomkais and the Ikkats which had their very own hay days too. Do you recall sisters?" The petite saree enquired.

The Kanchivaram pattu sarees too shook their heads in agreement. They were abundant in number. Amma was a hoarder, if one could call her that. She used to love collecting sarees, irrespective of whether she got an occasion to drape them or not.

"Do you know girls", said the Queen? "I have seen her ogle at our peers. The vibrant shades, colors and the soft feel used to make her eyes twinkle. Shopping in Chennai was never complete without barging into the silk section and coming us with a barrage of 'us' sister sarees. I have been her constant companion during the doll festival of Gollu each year. She used to take time draping 'US' types. We are heavy you see. Amma used to lovingly wrap us around, adorn bangles on her hands, put the beautiful jhimki kammals and wear her nose pin in pride. She was the picture of resplendence, the cynosure of all eyes at any social event. She used to love us for that affable fragrance of the sandalwood, the Kumkum and the divine Vibhuti, that we brought upon us after each wear. In fact, she used to smell us often to catch that waft of the Jasmine scent, the flowers which she used to adorn her hair with", the Queen Bee reminisced.

Each story brought about a wave of nostalgia in the other sarees. They never acted as each other's nemesis as Amma's sunshine splurged on them in the most ubiquitous manner possible. Every saree was dear to her and every shade appealed to her. The fragrance of each saree spoke volumes to her restless heart. Oh, the strange loving relationship that they shared.

The Kasavu set sarees, the Assamese Mekhala, The Jamdani and the famous Calcutta Banarasi were treasured as fondly as the others in the cupboard. She had no favorites. Most of the times, she wouldn't wash these sarees as their smell and fragrance would remind her of the occasion to which she had worn these sarees. Each saree would be worn and then neatly folded immaculately to preserve their indelible fragrance. Such was Amma's obsession with her sarees.

Amma now, had severe health issues. She swaddled an empty nest. She was alone most of the times. Her caretaker had neatly folded these in her room and locked them up. It seemed like eternity to these beauties. Their glory was lost forever. Amma couldn't wear anything except nighties and comfortable gowns these days. Her Alzheimer's was also getting the better of her. She lost track of time and of her cherished companions.

"Creak, Creak!", as the sound of the old wooden floor came nearer, the sarees looked on anxiously at the intruder.

All of a sudden, Amma opened the cupboard. She was lucid today, as is the case with dementia patients. She had suddenly remembered her treasure chest and had come slowly with the aid of her walker.

As she opened the cupboard, her eyes welled up. Memories of yesteryears came rushing back and Amma broke down. The sarees did not feel ostracized any longer. They had been freed from their languishment at last. Amma held each saree in her hand and took in their dormant fragrances, let it linger for some time. She was thus transported into her old world again after decades, it seemed.

"Phew! That was some blog that I penned", thought

Asmita! "I really hope I win this time. These are not fictional and I wish I could exhibit my Amma's sarees to the world, as an ode to her golden days. Well, even if I don't make it to the top blogger's list, yet this blog has served as a tribute to the hundreds of sarees lying in the adjacent room." She looked lovingly at Amma, now fast asleep on the cot.

On that note, Asmita turned away from her laptop. However, something struck her. It was a spur of the moment idea that struck her. She rushed to the old cupboard. There they were, staring at her lassitude, in all their evergreen glory. She was mesmerized at Amma's collection. The fragrances of each saree were different. Each one spoke volumes about their individual saga. She took her time to relish the beauty of each of these sarees. Such a collection deserved to be paraded in full glory to the world. Amma's story had to be told not only by way of a blog or a write up but also had to be presented across visually to make a lasting impression. What better way to do that than wear each saree and achieve what she had desired to in the first place!

Well, no more negligence, she decided and went back to her laptop, opened a new document and typed: 365 SAREES FOR 365 DAYS!

It was Saree time!

"We would request Asmita Iyer to come onto the stage to receive her trophy", reverberated the voices in her head. As the focus light shone on her, her petite silhouette was enhanced in full glory. She came out of her reverie. It had been exactly a year since her work was published. It had received rave reviews. The story of her mother, the story of those six yards of elegance and the story of a young woman who endeavored to bring justice to the yesteryear pomp and elan. She had finally achieved what she had set out to. The archaic story had finally made its way into innumerable hearts. People had fallen in love with the narrative and the author. They had flocked tonight to see the mysterious lady of the moment.

As Asmita made her way through the cheering crowds and the thundering applauses, her eyes were moist and her heart brimmed with pride. She walked up the podium, made her way into the limelight and clasped the trophy firmly. She glanced at the frail figure looking at her across the stage. She held up the trophy with both her hands and said lovingly - "Amma, this one is for you."

Amal Behbehani

Amal Behbehani is a Kuwaiti writer, who currently works at the American University of Kuwait. Her workplace is also where she completed her undergraduate studies in English Literature in 2011. In 2013, she completed her masters degree in Business Administration at Gulf University for Science and Technology.

While she dreams of writing, she fills her time with playing PokemonGo and rewatching New Girl with her sister. If not for the pandemic, you would find her traveling with her family, her favorite stop being Barnes and Nobles in the States, and comic book stores to check out with her brother. For now, she boroughs in her room, using this time to catch up on her reading and writing.

Amal has been writing short stories since her teenage years, entering some competitions during university years. Her stories mostly fall under fantasy and young adult. Her parents keep her motivated to expand her writing universe. This is Amal's attempt at getting back into writing.

Ananya Madhu

Ananya Madhu was born in Kerala, India and brought up in Bangalore. She did her schooling in Kendriya Vidyalaya in Bangalore. She started reading books at the age of twelve. The very first book that got her into reading was Pride and Prejudice by Jane Austen. Since then, she has gobbled up more books than she can remember. At the age of fifteen she found herself writing stories and poems as a hobby.

Now you can find her writing whenever she has free time. She hopes to own a big library filled with her favorite books in the future. Currently she is doing her engineering in Bangalore. You can always find her nose in a book.

Anushka Somavanshi

Anushka Somavanshi was born in Bhopal, Madhya Pradesh in a household where reading and writing was encouraged with great enthusiasm. So, she spent her childhood devouring everything from Goosebumps to Anne Frank.

For college, she opted to study Electrical Engineering (a far cry from literature- she knows) but pursued her writing dream through freelancing. She worked as a social media manager for a blogging business where she additionally wrote for them as well.

Being an avid Stephen King fan and horror buff, she wrote extensively in the same genre for magazines and competitions. She draws inspiration from books like 1922, In the Tall Grass, Gone Girl, and Bluebeard.

Her dream is to publish her own psychological thriller one day that creates a huge wave in the literary community.

She currently lives in Mumbai, Maharashtra with her parents, older sister, and thankfully, no pets.

Anushree Bose

Anushree Bose is a clinical researcher specializing in the scientific study of severe mental disorders like Schizophrenia. She has a PhD in Psychiatry and a Master's degree in Psychology. She has over fifty scientific journal publications to her credit and is peer reviewer for several Psychiatry journals.

Beyond academics, she likes to read, write and wonder about the human nature, something she explores through poetry and fiction. Her stories and poems feature in several published and upcoming anthologies: Everything Changes After that: 25 Women, 25 Stories (eShe Stort Story Contest Win), Through the Looking Glass - Indie Blu(e) publishing (in preparation), eShe Lockdown poetry Contest 2020 (September Issue), Songs of Peace: World's Biggest Anthology of Contemporary Poetry 2020, and Aatish-2.

She has contributed to Active Muse, Muse India, Berlin ArtParasite, and Spark India.

You can find her at:

Instagram: @byanushreebose

Facebook: https://www.facebook.com/anushree.bose.35

Aparna Arvind

Aparna, a mother, facilitator, author and an enthusiast loves to read, watch experience and write almost everything about what this magnificent life offers to us! She manifests her thoughts, ideas and opinions through writing. Her published kindle novel La Visit and her blog penflock.blogspot.com is a proof for the same.

Having a healthy and positive outlook about the society, Aparna draws her stories and inspirations from her family and her immediate surroundings. The varied opinions of the people she is acquianted with, their contradictory actions, controversial conversations and their different perspectives followed by the interesting narratives provides a plethora of choices for her writing. She is a passionate writer who pens every emotion and every detail into an interesting account!

Cara Finegan

Cara Finegan comes from Newry in Northern Ireland, right on the border. She graduated with a B.Ed Hons degree in English and Drama in 1995 and has been a Primary School teacher ever since. She has three children and surrounds herself with as many wonderfully wicked women as she possibly can. These women manage to keep her sane.

Cara has written stories and poems from a young age but put writing on hold for a number of years to follow her dream of becoming a burlesque and pole performer. She opened a dance studio and still has her own Burlesque dance troupe. After a few detouring years in dance she decided to spend more time on her writing.

Her first novel *Don't Call Me Baby*, a domestic noir, is currently agented by Alice Lutyens from Curtis Brown Literary Agency.

Cara is now working on her fourth novel and enjoys trying to use her many travel experiences as a back drop for her writing. As she is a lover of crime fiction and psychological thrillers her stories tend to have dark undercurrents. Usually, however, the female characters come out on top.

Chrissy Kett

Chrissy Kett is a London-based writer whose background is in musical theatre, having trained at The Italia Conti Academy of Performing Arts. She has performed in venues such as Sadler's Wells and The New Wimbledon Theatre, and has toured the UK extensively.

Over the last fourteen years she has also gained extensive experience in teaching, directing, choreographing, and facilitating workshops for all age groups. She continues to teach 4 - 18-year-olds at The Kett School of Speech and Drama, and she also enjoys delivering "Bringing Books to Life" and "Poetry in Motion" dance workshops for West End In Schools. Along the way, she has discovered that the pride that comes with helping a student develop their skills is far greater than the thrill of being on stage.

Having spent many years performing and teaching other people's work, she decided it was time she wrote some material of her own. She sat down, drank some coffee, and got to work (she finds that not much work gets done without coffee).

She was slightly surprised when she finished her first novel, and even more so now that she's writing the third of the trilogy, but looking back, she's realized she's been telling stories ever since she was small (or smaller – she still hasn't reached five foot). Perhaps she didn't realize it at the time, because she tended to act them out rather than write them down. Kids at school always wanted to play in her imaginary worlds at break times, and the adults always wanted to listen to her stories at Christmas (fully-staged performances in the lounge, obviously).

She now writes poetry, children's and YA fiction, and was thrilled when her verse Centennial Christmas won The Sloane Square Carol Competition. She would like to thank all of the WriteFluence team for giving fledging writers a voice, and the inspiration to keep on writing (even when there are days when none of her imaginary friends will talk to her and she finds herself staring at a blank page).

When she's not teaching, she can usually be found in coffee shops, writing and sipping a latté. When the UK comes out of lockdown, she can't wait to get back to writing and people watching, with coffee in hand.

Speaking of lockdown, for anyone working with children and young people, mental health awareness is of the utmost importance, and is something that Chrissy feels very passionately about.

In 2010 she worked for Ape Theatre Company, for a Theatre in Education tour delivering both performances and workshops for KS3 based on Road Safety and Anti-Bullying. She has also been the face of a "CyberMentors" campaign: "Don't suffer in silence."

Her short story holds young people at the front of her mind as she takes a sharp look at the UK's "tick-box" approach to learning.

Fía Ruve

Fía Ruve is a Latin American author born in Costa Rica. Throughout her life, she has been profoundly involved with diverse forms of art such as dancing, music, drawing, writing and painting; however, in writing she found her true inspiration.

During her adult life, she has been studying in multiple universities fields related to literature. She has also explored other interests like interculturality and communication due to her desire to interact with other places, people, languages, and cultures.

Fía writes fiction as well as poetry and producing new, creative, and meaningful texts is one of the main passions in her life. With her writing, she strives for people to question and generate their own meanings through her words. She aspires for her writings to express herself while relating and becoming what the reader needs or wants to see, even if they do not notice it.

Fiona Ballard

Fiona Ballard grew up in Hampshire and Malaya. She successfully combined motherhood with an NHS career spanning twenty five years. Fiona's life experiences have contributed hugely to the depth and substance of her writing. Her creative writing journey began with a gift of an entry fee to enter a story writing competition.

To date she has written ten short stories and one novel, a complete mixture of Adult and Young Adult fiction. Married now for nearly forty years she has two grown up married sons and one delightful grandchild.

Fiona belongs to a local Writers Hub which offers an eclectic mix of authors, courses, blogs, and opportunities for reviews. In between writing stories Fiona enjoys travelling, swimming, international cookery and dog walking.

Gowri Bhargav

Gowri Bhargav is a certified storyteller from Chennai. An Engineering graduate who is highly interested in arts, she has always had the passion to tell stories. Several storytelling workshops and events are being regularly conducted by her for the benefit of school children.

She has also contributed for "Talking Stories Radio" - a programme dedicated to the art of storytelling by East London radio. "BTB storyteller of the year 2020" was recently awarded to her by the jury panel of "Beyond the Box" Gowri is a voracious reader who loves getting lost in the world of books.

Writing is a form of catharsis for her and she enjoys weaving words into poems, micro tales, short stories and blogs. She has won several online contests conducted by prestigious literary groups. Her works have been featured and published in various online portals, literary magazines and journals. She has also co-authored several anthologies.

Iravati Kamat

Iravati is an engineer and a social worker from Maharashtra, India. Although she has been writing creatively since childhood, story writing started in one blissful and standstill moment at a Monastery in Leh, India. Since then, Iravati and her writing have travelled together a lot, both growing up together. In most of her stories, she likes to capture untapped emotions that often go unnoticed as we go on with our day.

Writing started out as a way of letting out her thoughts and observations. Now, she is losing herself in the art form and wants to explore it more as a medium of social impact. While working as a social worker and challenging the status quo around her and within her, her writing becomes her best aid and her fortress of solitude. Her areas of passion are mental health and gender.

Isabella Jeong

Isabella Jeong is the author of The Guest, one of the short stories in Wafting Earthy; and is a newly published writer. She graduated high school in 2020 and is currently on a gap year to explore her passion for literature. She intends to finish her next short story by the end of 2021.

Her favorite reads are: The Stranger by Albert Camus, Hamlet by William Shakespeare, A Farewell to Arms by Ernest Hemingway, The Sorrows of Young Werther by Wolfgang von Goethe, You are the Apple of My Eye by Giddens Ko. She loves reading fiction in any genre. Her favorite genre to write is romance.

Writing for Penfluenza, Isabella says: Writing for this theme provided an opportunity to identify what I need to work on in the future!

Kathrin Spinnler

Kathrin Spinnler always made up stories and wrote them down as a child. But after she graduated from university, she turned to teaching rather than writing. Only recently having focused more on this passion again, she is now writing consistently every day and submitting her stories to magazines and competitions. In the future, she hopes to write a longer novel. She calls herself a writer who never gives up.

She loves both reading and writing romance and adventure stories. Writing for Penfluenza she says: "I loved exploring 'fragrance' because smell can often get overpowered by the other senses in writing. It's an unusual topic and I did quite a lot of preparation work, researching fragrance words and methods of writing about smell. This is one of my favourite aspects of doing competitions with prompts: you get to learn more about the art of writing and you broaden your horizons."

Lavanya Girish

Lavanya Girish is an Educational Facilitator by profession. Having dabbled in the Banking and Financial Services Industry, she found her true calling in the writing arena. She has a flair for creative writing and participating in debates and elocutions from her childhood days. She wrote her first prose while she was in college. Thereafter, her forte has been writing poetry and short fictional stories.

Lavanya has always endeavored to hone her writing skills over time and these efforts have reaped immense benefits. She is also a blogger in numerous platforms and has got wide recognition in the blogosphere. She is associated with esteemed platforms such as Momspresso, The Pink Comrade and Write fluence wherein she has contributed poems, blogs and several write ups in different genres. She would like to summarize herself in a line – JACK of all Trades, Master of None. With hobbies spanning from painting, reading, listening to music and travelling she has truly found joy in all her pursuits. Although not religious, she is extremely spiritual and believes in the strength of the Almighty to guide her through thick and thin. Her works often reflect her ideologies and aspirations.

Lavanya attempts to unravel the mysteries of a Woman's mind through this story. This is one tale which most of us can resonate with. The need for feeling desirable and wanted is there in every woman and the vulnerability that comes with lack of recognition often drives a woman in a tangential direction. The story attempts to highlight the desire of the woman to feel appreciated and wanted. The story also attempts to highlight the sacrifice that a woman undergoes to make sure her family has her undivided time and attention. Through her simplistic manner of writing, she brings to detail small nuances of everyday life.

Linda Hibbin

Linda Hibbin is a mosaic artist living near the English Essex coast.

She has squiggled a few light-hearted lines of poetry over the years, usually to let off steam as a housewife and mother, and more recently wrote and illustrated stories for her granddaughter about the magical adventures of her unruly terrier, Poppy.

Linda became seriously interested, addicted might be a better word, in writing flash fiction and short stories when sharing her work for the first time, with other writers, during online creative writing courses in 2020.

Much of her work is inspired by her own life experiences. Some are thought-provoking, many reflect the humorous side of life or are pure fantasy.

Her work has been accepted by a number of writer websites and the elation experienced seeing her words in print is on a par with a sky-dive on her 65th birthday.

Louisa Ellemind

Louisa Ellemind is a writer, singer / songwriter and psychology student. Her first novel, The Hunted, a sci-fi / fantasy adventure about sisterhood and finding your identity, was published in 2019. She loves writing about strange people in strange worlds. She's currently working on her first middle grade novel, The Seers Sisters, a book about witches, boarding school, sisterhood, and confidence.

Ellemind is a survivor of depression and believes in spreading kindness and understanding. She lives in Oldenburg, Germany, with her two invisible ghost cats.

Catch up with her on louisaellemind.com or on Twitter at @LouiLae Subscribe to her newsletter at louisaellemind.com/news

Nilanjana Banerjee

Nilanjana Banerjee is a collegian, pursuing Honours in English.

Keats, coffee and cheese are necessities to her. She pours her feelings in writing, most of which are impromptu. Her experimentation with words began when she was fourteen.

She had been trapped in a writer's block for four years until one day when a door of inspiration was opened to her by an unknown Muse, waking a side of her creativity that was asleep for eons.

Banerjee is fascinated by thrillers. However, she tastes various flavours of literature and enjoys them. Some of her favourite authors are Charles Dickens, Agatha Christie, P.G. Wodehouse and Stephen King.

She is usually engaged in composing poetry. The contest of Penflueza organised by WriteFluence gave her an opportunity to explore the author in her. Her inclination towards thriller shaped her story and incorporated the unique theme of "fragrance" into it from an unexpected angle.

Banerjee finds solace in the fact that her words can finally speak instead of remaining confined within the bounds of her mind.

Rohan Swamy

Indian-born writer Rohan Swamy, lives and works in Dublin, Ireland; and began writing in 2002. A former journalist, he has tried to combine the art of story telling with journalistic trends and enjoys writing stories based on current socio-political trends across the world.

A graduate of Trinity College, Dublin, Rohan has worked as a journalist in India with the Indian Express Newspapers and with NDTV before moving on to writing fiction full-time. He has been a contributing writer during his university days with the oldest student newspaper publications in Ireland – The University Times and Trinity News, writing on student life, and issues connected to Irish and American politics. In addition, he wrote a column called 'After Thought' for Sakaal Times in Pune, in 2017. As a short story writer, his first published stories appeared in the Urban Shots anthologies – Crossroads and The Love Collection, in 2012 respectively. In Europe he has been published in 'College Green' and 'The Attic' - magazines published by the Trinity College Dublin Press.

On days when he is not writing he prefers to go hiking, photographing and exploring the Irish countryside. He also divides time between running, playing the harmonica and cooking – activities that help him find sanity in a fast changing world.

Rupsa Das

Rupsa Das was born in Kolkata, West Bengal. She's 20, and currently pursuing computer science engineering. Her mother introduced her to books from a tender age, and she soon discovered the joy of reading. From Bengali to English books, she loved reading them all.

Her teen life was mostly spent in dystopian fiction worlds, from Camp Half-Blood to Panem. After finishing high school from Gokhale Memorial Girls' School in Kolkata, she took up engineering in Haldia Institute of Technology in 2019. Coding had been her interest for a long time, alongside reading and writing fiction.

She hopes to continue writing fiction, alongside her career in the technical field.

Santhini Govindan

Santhini Govindan is a widely published, award-winning author of children's literature in English. She has written more than fifty books for children of all ages, and her work includes poetry, picture books, and short stories. Santhini has been awarded two Fellowships in Literature from the Ministry of Human Resource Development, Department of Culture, Government of India for research projects connected to children's literature in India.

In October 2018, she was awarded a Lok-Sabha Fellowship to write a book to introduce children to the role and function of the Indian parliament.

Santhini Govindan has authored and edited several English language readers that are widely used in schools across India, the Middle East and South East Asia, and has taught Creative Writing at the under-graduate level at Mumbai University. She loves animals and enjoys doing amigurumi, embroidery and gardening, and is an inveterate collector of bells and angels.

Shilpa Keshav

Shilpa was born and brought up in Mumbai, India. Her father served as a Scientific Officer in the reputed Central Government firm, BARC for 35 years. A gold medallist in MSc (Analytical Chemistry), she worked as a Research Associate in a Multinational Pharmaceutical company before getting married and relocating to Dubai, UAE. Her father introduced her to books in her childhood and that's when her love for reading and writing began. She would write short stories for various children's monthly magazines. Later, as her studies took priority, writing took a back seat. Writing has always been her first love.

She has published short stories on various online platforms and has won on several occasions. PenFluenza is her first stint at getting published. Her brother, Mr. Sudeep Satheesan is an author too, and his writings encourage her immensely. Apart from writing and reading, she loves listening to music and watching movies. She resides in Dubai with her husband and two adorable kids, who make sure that she is charged up all the time under all circumstances.

Sneha Acharekar

Sneha Acharekar is a passionate logophile, an avid reader, a complete movie buff and a singer in places that reverberate. In that order. She is a writer by passion and profession; and has been writing fiction since her school days – stories and poems for her school magazine.

An active blogger and poetess on various online sites, her articles have made it to the featured lists on various online platforms as Momspresso, Women's Web and YourQuote. She is an avid Chetan Bhagat fan for the love of the simplicity in his writings – Five Point Someone and Two States being her favourite works of the author. The Harry Potter series follows as her next favourite book and she loves reading Dean Koontz and Shobha De. A voracious reader since school days, with the constant thought about having just a few years in hand to complete school and too many books to go from the library... she would gulp down every Enid Blyton book in The Famous Five series during zero periods in school. She wrote her first story of about ten thousand plus odd words during her ninth grade which she still treasures as her motivation to write.

As of today, Acharekar has three published books to her name. Based on the genre of dark romance, her first fiction novel Faith, Fate and a Fairytale (2017) is the closest to her heart. Her first book in the non-fiction genre – Let Go, Yet Glow – was published in January 2014 under a pseudonym KaTHaa. Purple Winters (2020) is the third of her books which is a collection of 150 free verses. Her poems are also published in 'Spent', a poetry compilation by WriteFluence published in 2021.

Acharekar came up with Stories by Sneha in 2020 – a podcast that plays on all podcasting channels viz. AnchorFM, Spotify, Apple Podcasts, Google Podcasts, Hubhopper, KukuFM, RadioPublic, Castbox, Breaker, PocketCasts, Overcast, to name a few. The podcast features short-stories written and narrated by Acharekar; with the entire audio experience and ambience conceptualised and created by her individually; and has successfully crossed over 40k listens overall – that being a good number considering the span and the popularity of the medium of podcasts with Indian listeners.

Acharekar calls herself resilient because she has learnt it the hard way through many life challenges. Yet, her faith remains strong in the doctrine of Agathism – all things tend towards ultimate good. Acharekar considers herself lucky to have supportive parents, a loveable spouse and an adorable daughter; and further blessed to have been born and brought up in Mumbai.

When she is not writing, Acharekar loves to create digital illustrations, listen to music, explore digital apps or sing karaoke.

She's currently working on content for Season 2 of Stories by Sneha that will begin sometime soon in 2021. If you're a writer and want your story to reach a relatively large listener's base, reach out to her on her Instagram handle @the.agathist

Sohini Roy

Sohini Roy is a nineteen-year-old, college student, living in Kolkata, West Bengal. She graduated from South Point High School in the year 2019, and now, aspires to be a successful author and an artist. She has always dreamt of enwrapping cold and dark minds in the warmth of the colours of her imagination.

She started writing as an escape from the monotony and stress, but gradually it built into something stronger where the words were not only to comfort her, but also those around her. Roy hopes someone in some unnoticed corner of this huge world, can find a friend, a solace through her words.

Swathi H.

Swathi H., a literature student exploring the endless possibilities of language, was born and brought up in Kochi. She lives with her parents, grandmother, sister, and pet fish Flake.

Being the kid who jotted down newly-learned words, the enticing charm of words held her fancy. Soon like every other reader, she was drawn into the world of books. Each book showed her the magic of words to move, inspire and transform; a talent that rests with the writer. Thus began the experiment of stringing together words of her own.

Her writing is weaved with threads of reality that often leave you in wonder. When not writing, you can find her at a used bookstore or laughing at her jokes (sometimes both). As long as there is coffee in the cup and a notepad, she is ready to take on the world.

Tanvi Kashyap

Tanvi Kashyap was born in the city of Chandigarh, India, in a middle-class family, her mother a homemaker and her father, a librarian. As a child, whenever she fell ill, her father would often bring story books for her to read. Hence, her introvert self-found refuge in the shelter of books. Thus, fantasy and imagination never left her side. The stories she loved reading the most were those which were like food for the soul. 'Chicken soup for the soul' was her constant companion during the teenage years. She ventured into the world of the Harry Potter series just to get lost in the riveting account of the life of a wizard. Thus, started her journey as a writer, who wanted to express the beauty of the world, touch the hearts of millions of people and transform their lives with the magic of her words.

However, with time and the daily life responsibilities, the passion for writing just faded away. Years later, when she saw this astounding blog 'WriteFluence', on Instagram, encouraging amateur writers to follow their passion. She wrote her first short story 'Memaroma' which was amongst the top five short stories of an international short story writing contest called PenFluenza, an initiative of WriteFluence, an upcoming platform for budding writers. Writing has become an essential part of her life, a catharsis, an opportunity to express herself to the rest of the world.

Udita Mukherjee

Udita Mukherjee resides in the nostalgia wafting from Kolkata. She completed her B.Sc. in Economics from Presidency University in 2020. Her short story 'The Lemon and the Window' was selected for the March 2021 issue of Kloud9 whose editor-in-chief is Ruskin Bond. The first play she wrote titled Appendix was selected by Bombay Theatre Company for The Theatre Project 2020 and can be found in the IGTV section of their Instagram page. One of her poems was amongst the top ten entries for a magazine published by Author's Ink Publications.

Her entry for WriteFluence's Femmefluenza, a contest celebrating womanhood and recognizing its struggles, was one of the winners. Blue Trunk Press has published a short story of hers in their anthology Square One. Another of her poems was picked by The Write Order for their book of poetry, Panacea.

She is enthusiastic about bubble wrap and stories, in no particular order. She hopes to spread positivity and acceptance cloaked in dark humor through her writing. Virginia Woolf and Oscar Wilde have her heart, Roald Dahl and Enid Blyton have her soul.

Varsha Murthy

Born and raised in Bangalore, Varsha Murthy is 19 years old, just starting out on her writing journey.

Currently pursuing a degree in Psychology, English Literature and Communications, she spends her free time with her two dogs. Her hobbies mostly involve reading fanfiction, listening to k-pop and scrolling through social media.

Reading for her has always been an escape from day to day life and writing started off as just another facet of the same. She writes so she can turn off everything happening in her own life and focus on her characters instead. She prefers writing short stories most and hopes that through her writing, she can provide an escape to her readers as well.

Vibhuti Bhandarkar

Vibhuti Bhandarkar started her career in 2004 as a professionally qualified Commercial Artist and freelance English Copywriter for top brands and Ad' agencies in Pune.

Ever since, she has constantly experimented with different areas of her expertise and explored her creative genius.

She has contributed features for many publications like the TOI supplements, Femina, etc.

She has also been a serial entrepreneur in the field of Fine Art; right from running her own Art Gallery to designing interiors of Pubs, from winning recognition for her hand-painted fashion accessories to illustrating book cover designs- she's dabbled in it all!

Vibhuti's restless creative genes have never allowed her to put her feet up and relax, ever! In 2009 she received accolade as an avid creative blogger, which eventually helped her strike off one goal on her bucket list- becoming a published writer before turning 30. Her maiden collection of short stories, 'Not Totally Unbelievable' was published in 2011, and till date many of her short stories have been published in anthologies like the Chicken Soup for the Soul, and in E-magazines.

Presently, Vibhuti is working on a Romantic Suspense novella and a Historical Fiction Novel, aspiring to be a novelist some day!

***Apart from winning the position for her short story in Wafting Earthy, she also won the Create-a-Cover contest associated with PenFluenza to create and design the book cover for Wafting Earthy!

Victoria Fenwick

Victoria Fenwick is an English and Drama teacher from Ashington, Northumberland. She has lived in Newcastle upon Tyne, Milan and Bangkok, and has flown a plane, been on Ghanian TV and once ate pork pies with Alan Shearer. She is also a triplet.

Aged 8, she completed her first original novella, an eponymous piece about an anthropomorphic dog on a dog planet titled 'Squishy'. The first (and only) edition was self published on a home printer and can be found pride of place at her mother's home at the bottom of a nondescript box in a loft.

Her second project was a rip off of Lemony Snicket's 'A Series of Unfortunate Events' and didn't even make it to the printer. Since then, she has been honing her craft through practising, teaching and lots of reading. As well as short stories, she enjoys writing poetry and playwriting. She studied English Literature and Philosophy at Newcastle University where she also completed a master's degree in Creative Writing. She is an avid skier, dabbles in drawing and still loves dogs.

Vignesh Sivasankar

Vignesh Siva Sankar always believes writing is the only way human civilization has evolved. He hopes that human imagination has no bounds, and there is no greater power than a passionate writer penning down his or her creativity. As a child, he was always attracted to stories. He was not introduced to books early on but was inclined to watching cinema and became a movie buff. The only hero he admired was the STORY.

Soon, when books came into his life, writing became his friend and now he has developed an intimate relationship with art. To earn the bucks during the day he does sales, marketing, leadership, and team management. His life also has a chapter on failed entrepreneurship. At night, he's in his Lala land of creating his universe sprawling with characters he invents. An engineer and a management graduate, he's an alumnus of Anna University, Symbiosis University, Indian Institute of Management Calcutta, and EDII.

A published author, he writes in diverse genres of fiction and non-fiction. Currently, he's more into horror tales! Vignesh has published an essay in the Book "Youth as Nation Builders" by Lab Academia publishers.

He is a winner of a published article presented in the International Conference on Literature and Technology by Literoma Publications.

He has another essay published in Medium - 2060.C.E

- Post-Covid-19.

He won the All India Literature Competition 2019-20 for Short story "Neerpuri" - Published online in Creative Post.

He has also participated and published a short story online for "Story Mirror" for the short story "Pain is Ok."

He has published a horror short story in Kindle form, "Hypnagogic," via Half-baked beans.

Vignesh has also had his short stories published as an author in Notion Press.

Another short story of his was published in "Perspectives of Hope" anthology by Lab Academia "Extra Ordinary Gentleman."

His short story 'The Rickshaw Puller' was shortlisted as the best one in 'Word weavers Contest 2020.'

Vishaal Pathak

Vishaal Pathak was born in Lucknow, India in a middle-class family. Curious yet introverted, he spent his time taking apart toy machines and putting them back together. His parents saw an Engineer in him, and before he knew it, he was chasing the conventional Indian dream.

Apart from a game of cricket each evening, books were his only friend for the most part. School books during the week and story books during the weekend. In seventh grade, he convinced his school librarian to issue the only volume of Sherlock Holmes in his name indefinitely because the mammoth book of complete works was too big to finish in a week, too heavy to carry to school every week for reissuance and too tempting to give up. When he still couldn't finish them, his parents eventually bought him a copy. To this date, the collection lies unfinished in his personal library and he hopes to revisit the stories someday.

By high-school, the occasional cricket and the odd story books were gone. All that was left was academic books. All through his engineering at National Institute of Technology, Allahabad and later MBA from Indian Institute of Management, Kozhikode, he rarely had the chance to pick up books, except maybe for a gift or a talked-about Booker of the year. Although, occasionally, he'd contribute with the pen to the institute's annual magazines. He was drowning in spreadsheets, wireframes and user stories when the unthinkable happened and brought the world to a screeching halt.

It was only around June 2020 when the situation got the better of him and he turned to writing, nearly full-time. Since then, he has self-published two small-length books (notably, "I Can, Sir!" based on the true story of his dear friend) and has a couple of short-stories published as part of anthologies. Writing, he believes, is medicine for the soul. The topics that pique his interest the most are time, memory and ethics.

Among his favorite books are 'Catcher in the Rye', 'To Kill a Mockingbird' and 'Never Let Me Go'. While currently writing short stories, he hopes someday to be able to write something of relevance – ambitious in both length and depth. When not writing, he can be found daydreaming or cycling.

Printed in Great Britain
by Amazon

61923113R00163